MACDOUGAL'S LUCK

MACDOUGAL'S LUCK

Betty McInnes

This first world edition published in Great Britain 2003 by
SEVERN HOUSE PUBLISHERS LTD of
9–15 High Street, Sutton, Surrey SM1 1DF.
This first world edition published in the USA 2003 by
SEVERN HOUSE PUBLISHERS INC of
595 Madison Avenue, New York, N.Y. 10022.

British Library Cataloguing in Publication Data

McInnes, Betty, 1928-
   MacDougal's luck
   1.   Women domestics - Fiction
   2.   Automobile repair shops - Fiction
   3.   Great Britain - Social life and customs - 1918-1945 - Fiction
   I.   Title
   823.9'14 [F]

   ISBN 0-7278-5943-9

Typeset by Palimpsest Book Production Ltd.,
Polmont, Stirlingshire, Scotland.
Printed and bound in Great Britain by
MPG Books Ltd., Bodmin, Cornwall.

For Ethel Connell, Ishbel's great-grandma

One

November the 16th 1918 was declared a public holiday to celebrate the signing of the Armistice. A street party was in full swing outside the Drill Hall on that Saturday afternoon, not far from Sir William Granton's London mansion. The women organizers had decided to hold the event out of doors if possible, because of the threat of influenza, which had reached epidemic proportions in London. Fortunately, the weather was kind and the day had dawned dry and quite mild.

Gracie MacDougal and the other children seated at tables in the old barrack square were well-mufflered and bonneted as a precaution, however. A pale sun shone on their bowed heads. Gracie quietly loosened her scarf as the vicar concluded a long-winded prayer, touching on war, peace, and the food laid before them. Gracie chorused a thankful 'Amen!' and opened her eyes.

Hillocks of sandwiches topped by paper Union Jacks made her quite faint with hunger. Her stomach had rumbled at an awkward moment during the prayer and the girl next to her had giggled while Gracie blushed. When the signal came to tuck in, she hardly knew what to choose. Little cards on sticks said 'Roast Beef' or 'Chicken', and 'Egg' or 'Tomato'. A tantalizing choice!

'Help yourself,' she said politely to the girl.

'Ta.' She grabbed a sandwich in each hand and wolfed them down hungrily. Gracie chose tomato and nibbled an

1

edge of bread with the crusts cut off. The girl's hunger ruined her appetite.

'You look after her, now, Gracie luv!' her mother had whispered before they started. 'Her East End school was bombed in 1917, poor lamb. She's lucky to be alive.'

Gracie eyed the girl, who was about thirteen, her own age. She longed to ask her about the bombing. Was she scared when the German bombers came? Was she injured, and did she have nightmares? I would! she thought.

'Pass the chicken,' the girl said.

Gracie obliged.

Gracie and her two older sisters had been fortunate considering the horrors this poor girl had faced. The MacDougal family occupied the chauffeur's flat above the coach-house attached to Sir William and Lady Granton's impressive mansion, and the only serious upset and disturbance to life had been their father's call-up to war and the bell on the kitchen wall which summoned Mum to Lady Frances Granton's bedside if the invalid lady took a bad turn in the night.

'Is that real tomato?' the girl asked.

'Yes, they're hothouse. My Grandma sells them on her barrow in Lambeth market.'

'Blimey! Is your Grandma on the straight and narrows?'

'Not 'arf!' Gracie laughed.

Her mum, Polly, was Cockney, and Gracie was familiar with Cockney rhyming slang. She admired her mother tremendously. Mum had known hard times, but retained a sense of humour. She said you should put bad times behind you and get on with living.

Gracie was glad the worst times were over, though Mum said 'armistice' only meant 'truce'. Both sides had agreed to stop fighting on the eleventh hour of the eleventh day of the eleventh month of 1918, to give politicians time to work out a solution.

At that moment Gracie's mum came out of the Drill Hall carrying two big jugs of milk. The tops were covered with butter muslin weighted with glass beads that tinkled pleasantly as she walked. She looked neat and pretty in a frilly pinafore over a red dress. Gracie warmed with pride, but as her mother approached along the lines of enamel mugs held out eagerly, Gracie noticed dark shadows beneath her eyes, as if she hadn't slept well.

Gracie knew why.

Their father had survived the war – but as a prisoner in a German prisoner of war camp. Joseph MacDougal's wife and daughters hadn't seen him for nearly three years, although a recent communication from the War Office promised he would be home soon. The Drill Hall must hold sad memories for Mum because Dad had trained as a soldier there before being called up in 1916 with the other forty-year-olds. He'd been taken prisoner soon after and she must've missed him terribly. His three daughters certainly had!

Gracie finished the sandwich, helped herself to roast beef and was offering tomato and egg to her companion when Mum arrived with the milk. She smiled at the East End girl. 'Our Gracie looking after you, luv? That's good.'

She moved on down the row of children and the girl stared after her.

'Cor, she's pretty. Is that your ma?'

Gracie glowed with pride. 'Yes, that's her. She made the jellies,' she added casually.

She'd been warned not to mention it but couldn't see why she shouldn't. Sir William had given Mum permission to borrow copper moulds that turned out jellies big as sandcastles. They stood wobbling on large dishes in the centre of the tables, patriotically striped raspberry red, blancmange white and blackberry blue.

'You're well-off, ain't yer?' the girl said.

3

'Who, me?'

Gracie had never considered the MacDougals well-off.

The Grantons were. Sir William was a stockbroker with a big London house, a sporting estate in Scotland, lovely motor cars and dozens of servants. Mum had been plain Polly Hawkins working as housemaid in the big house when she and Scottish Dad fell in love. Dad had been Sir William's coachman before becoming his chauffeur. Mum had also in the course of time been promoted to be Lady Frances's personal maid.

But, pondered Gracie, though the Grantons were so well-off, Lady Frances was in poor health and depended upon Mum to look after her, Sir William had a constant worried look and their only child, Sebastian, had spent all his schooldays at strict boarding schools he'd absolutely hated.

Well-off? Blimey! Compared to the Grantons, the Mac-Dougals' existence was a bed of roses.

The sandwich plates were empty. Scones and jam, and iced cakes had all disappeared, jelly and trifle dishes scraped clean. The East End girl sat back with a sigh.

'I'm full to bustin'. A spread like that must've cost a bob or two. Who's paying?'

'I don't know.'

Payment had never crossed Gracie's mind. Now she worried in case the inhabitants of Granton Mews were asked to foot the bill. Everyone was hard up, though the MacDougals never wanted for anything. She knew Mum's wages and the few shillings Gracie's older sisters, Rosie and Lily, earned would hardly pay for the jellies. The awful prospect of the pawn shop loomed.

When the tables were cleared and dirty dishes stacked in the Drill Hall kitchen, Gracie tackled her mother about who was picking up the tab.

'Sir William Granton,' Mum answered briefly.

'Why should he?'

'Why shouldn't he, girl?'

'Is he grateful for something?'

Mum looked exasperated. 'For heaven's sake, Grace, of course he's grateful! The man has a seventeen-year-old son who won't be called up to fight.'

'Sebastian wanted to. He told me so. He wanted to drive a tank right through the Germans.'

'More fool him! He shouldn't be putting warlike thoughts into a little girl's head. That boy's a troublemaker.'

Gracie was indignant. 'No, he's not! And I'm not a little girl. I'm almost fourteen.'

'Yes, I know,' Polly MacDougal said, tightening her lips.

Gracie had finished clearing up when her two sisters arrived in the hall all dolled up and smelling to high heaven of Californian Poppy. There was to be dancing in the Drill Hall that evening to round off the celebrations.

'Run along home and get dressed up, Gracie,' said Rosie, the eldest.

'I *am* dressed up.'

Lily, the middle one, chuckled. 'No, you're not, luvvie, you've got pudding on the bodice of your dress.'

It was true Gracie's dress had suffered at the street party, but she had decided a few stains wouldn't be noticed. Trust fussy Lily to spot them! Still, she had planned to ask Sebastian to do the polka with her, so maybe she should be spotless. She went in search of Grandma Hawkins.

Her grandmother reached for a store of hankies kept up her sleeve for such emergencies. She wet one at the tap and settled down to sponge her granddaughter.

'The tomato sandwiches were lovely, Grandma. A girl from the East End thought we were well-off.'

'So we are, ducks. Poor girl could spot quality, bless 'er

'eart. Freshest fruit an' veg in London on your grandpa's barrow.'

'Sir William Granton paid for everything, Gran. Mum says because he's grateful.'

'Everyone's grateful war's ended, Gracie luv.'

'The armistice is only temporary. Politicians make peace. That's more difficult than making war, Grandma.'

Liza Hawkins studied the child's serious face uneasily.

'Know what, Gracie? You're too clever by 'alf. Sharp as a bloomin' needle, you are, luvvie.'

'Gran, don't say that! Needles can hurt.'

'But we can't do without 'em, dearie!' Liza Hawkins said kindly, hugging her little granddaughter.

Sebastian Granton refused to dance the polka with Gracie.

'Sorry, old girl. No can do!'

The young man and his well-to-do friends had arrived noisily by car, bringing with them the latest rich man's toy, an elaborate and wonderful mahogany gramophone. When fully wound, music poured from the instrument's flaring horn, creating such a sensation that old Enoch, the fiddler, went off in a huff and Mr Jackson, the church organist, banged down the lid of the tinny old Drill Hall piano in utter frustration.

Sebastian examined the small stock of records.

'Sorry, Gracie. We have "Merry Widow", "No, No, Nanette", "Tiptoe Through the Tulips", "Turkey Trot" and Alexander's Ragtime Band. No polka.'

'Oh, I love ragtime, Mr Granton!' Rosie gushed.

Gracie scowled. Her sister had been hanging around Sebastian hopefully. She had a crush on him and had threatened Gracie with dire consequences if he found out she sold fruit and veg on Uncle Sid's barrow. Rosie might sound sugar-sweet and look pretty, but she could bellow louder than a Lambeth barrow-boy – and cuff a sister's ear quite painfully.

'Why don't you ask Sebastian to dance? That's what you're after, isn't it?' Gracie said.

'The thought never crossed my mind!' Rosie protested, looking daggers. 'I'm sure Mr Granton won't want to dance with me.'

'On the contrary,' he smiled gallantly, crooking an arm. 'May I have the pleasure?'

'Don't mind if I do.'

Gracie watched the two turkey-trotting. She took turns cranking the gramophone but soon wearied of that monotony. She counted the lovelorn youths mooning around her sister Lily. Lily was the beauty of the family. She was training to be a telephonist at the Post Office Telephone Exchange, and could speak in tones so genteel Gracie was convinced she'd marry a duke.

Grandma Hawkins said that though Lily was a beauty and Rosie a chip off the old Hawkins' block, Gracie had the lion's share of brains. Gracie watched Rosie one-stepping energetically with Sebastian while Lily flirted with a dozen adoring boys.

I'll settle for the brains, she thought.

The hall grew hotter and noisier as more young people flocked in before the Sabbath put a stop to the fun. The fiddler returned by popular request to eke out the gramophone records and Mr Jackson was back at the piano thumping away at the Lancers. Gracie put on coat and hat and slipped outside.

It was quiet in the street, the air chilly. There was a damp haze around gaslamps and a magical silver glitter from the moon. It was the sort of night anything could happen, but not air raids, thank goodness. Boy Scout messengers had sounded the last All Clear on tinny trumpets a week ago and Londoners had danced in the Underground.

And Dad will be home soon! Gracie gave a little skip for joy. She'd never been really, truly happy since her father went away. He'd left his wife and family reluctantly, unable to hide the tears. He'd left something else behind, too, entrusting Gracie with its care. She walked towards the mews. The former stables housed the Grantons' cars, amongst them a silver Rolls Royce, black landau and Sebastian's three-wheeled Morgan.

But Gracie's pride and joy was the racing car known to the family as 'MacDougal's Luck', the car her father had designed and built just before he left. Dad had trained with a Scottish blacksmith before he worked for Sir William and was a genius with engines.

Sebastian and Gracie were both fascinated by cars, which had created a firm bond. He maintained that Gracie knew more about engines than he did himself.

Well, perhaps, she admitted modestly. She'd followed her father around the workshop like his shadow since she was a toddler. Sebastian pretended to be jealous, but was secretly proud of her. The other girls he knew weren't remotely interested in cars.

Both youngsters were longing for Joseph MacDougal's return, but for different reasons. Sebastian needed Joseph's written permission to test drive the racing car at Brooklands track, opened in 1907 on Mr Locke-King's Weybridge estate.

Gracie yawned. She was tired. It had been a long day and she hadn't felt like dancing. She'd decided to go home and put the kettle on and wait for her mother and sisters to return. It would be fun to sit by the fireside later on and listen to their chatter over a cup of cocoa.

She opened the small wicket-gate in the large coach-house doors and went inside. The family used this entrance as a shortcut to the flat above. There was no need to switch on the light. Even by night the spacious interior was adequately lit by street lamps shining through the high windows.

Dad's car lay ahead of Gracie, shrouded in dust sheets, and on impulse she wriggled beneath the sheets and sat in the driving seat. She felt close to Dad in there, and the car evoked delightful memories.

She remembered when she was a tiny girl Dad had been forced to work secretly on a prototype of this model. He'd been a coachman then and Sir William had heartily disapproved of automobiles, which he said terrified the horses.

Sebastian was about seven at the time, and made a beeline for the mews whenever his horrible boarding school released him for the holidays. Dad had been experimenting with the engine at that stage and the early model had back-fired with an ear-splitting explosion which sent the horses into wild frenzy and tiny Gracie tumbling. Fortunately, she landed in the middle of a haybag.

'Wow! That was wizard,' Sebastian cheered, picking himself off the ground.

'Oh, michty, the bairn!' Dad rummaged in the hay for his beloved child and covered her dirty face with thankful kisses. One waxed tip of his luxuriant moustache had been burned clean off.

'Ignition not properly adjusted, Gracie. Spark ignited petrol fumes in the exhaust pipe, love, that's all,' he'd explained.

Sir William had heard the din and came storming in. 'What the devil's going on, MacDougal? You know I detest the internal combustion engine!'

Dad feared for his job then, but Gracie had saved the day. Recalling her mother's regular wash-day moan, scrubbing filthy oil-stained overalls, she'd piped up, 'Bloomin' blasted infernal 'bustion!'

Sir William had burst out laughing. 'Well, well, Joseph! Out of the mouths of babes, as they say!'

Shortly afterwards, Sir William had bought his first motor car, a gleaming product of the union between Charles Rolls and Frederick Royce . . .

Gracie smiled. She could picture her handsome father very clearly as she sat here, remembering the blue eyes that were mostly alive with laughter, but sometimes reflective and sad.

The hinges of the wicket gate squealed and someone came in. Mum most likely, wondering where she'd got to. Her mother called softly, 'Darling, are you there?'

To Gracie's surprise a man's voice answered. 'I'm here, Polly.'

There were footsteps, her mother's quick and light, the man's heavier coming from the far end. The two sounds met and there was silence. Gracie shrank in the seat, the leather icy against her spine.

'Have you been waiting long, dearest?' she heard her mother say.

'No, just arrived. Difficult to get away, Poll. You know how it is.'

'I know.'

The voice came breathlessly quick, as if they stood close together. But surely her mother would not—

'Any news?' the man demanded.

'Yes . . .' Her mother began sobbing quietly. Gracie couldn't believe it. Her brave mum in tears! 'They've released Joseph now. He could be home any day.'

'You must tell him about us, Polly!'

'No, I couldn't do that to him, after all he's been through. It would be cruel.'

'Look, darling, we didn't want to fall in love, but it happened and those we care about will be hurt. That's inevitable.'

'Not if we fight it. Not if we don't meet.'

'But that's impossible, dear!'

'Difficult, not impossible.'

'Polly dear, please don't do this! Three years is a long time. Joseph may have changed out of all recognition. You could find yourself married to a stranger.'

'I'll be the stranger in our marriage, not him,' she said sadly. There was a longish silence, then Gracie heard him sigh.

'Is it really over, Polly?'

'Yes. We knew from the start it was wrong. Your poor wife—'

'Wait! don't go yet. Kiss me, Polly!'

'And weaken? No, William. I daren't.'

The door closed.

But who was William . . . ?

Sir William Granton, of course!

The shock hit Gracie with such force it brought tears to her eyes. The clues had all been there once you knew where to look. This love affair was the real reason why they'd never lacked for anything since Dad went away. Sir William had provided the food and nice clothes, the payment of doctor's bills when needed. And today, the street party, the wonderful jellies had only happened because Mum had been unfaithful!

Maybe she should have suspected something was wrong, but it had never entered her head. Sir William was a rich man and her mother's employer. Gracie had never wondered why he should be so caring; she'd just taken it for granted.

She crouched shivering in the cold leather seat, terrified to move a muscle in case he heard her. She tried to make sense of what her mother and this man had done, but the more she thought about it, the worse it became.

Mum was a married woman and Sir William had a lovely wife. Mum was Lady Frances's favourite maidservant and nurse. She tended the sick lady daily, read to her, nursed her through bad turns, made her laugh with Cockney humour. And all the time she was deceiving poor Lady Granton, and deceiving Dad!

How could the mother Gracie loved and admired be so downright wicked? It was beyond comprehension.

The man had walked away to the back of the mews. There was a doorway there which led into the gardens. His footsteps sounded heavy, like an old man's. Gracie heard the door close and realized she was alone with her thoughts. To be all alone was even more painful.

What will I do? Who can I turn to? Who can I tell? she asked herself frantically.

Reason supplied the answers. There was nothing she could do and nobody to turn to. She couldn't accuse Mum because the harm was already done and that would make it worse. There was nobody she could tell, not Dad or her sisters; and certainly not Sebastian, her best friend.

Gracie gave a small, wounded whimper. She was too young to have such knowledge thrust upon her. It weighed her down so that she felt aged and heavy as she crawled out from under the dustsheets and made her way slowly upstairs to the flat.

There was no thought now of boiling a kettle and waiting up for her sisters; it was all she could do to undress and crawl shakily into bed. She didn't bother to light the night light sitting in a saucer of water to ward off bad dreams. The nightmare was already there, inside her head.

Later on, Mum came quietly into the room and lit the night light, then sat by the bed. 'Gracie, are you awake?'

She thought of feigning sleep, but she'd had enough of lies.

'Yes.'

'Are you feeling all right, luvvie?'

'No, I'm not.'

Mum put a hand anxiously on Gracie's brow.

'Does your head hurt, dear?'

'Yes.'

If only her mother knew how much it hurt, if only she knew the pain she'd caused! Gracie read the fear in her mother's eyes.

Influenza!

The 'flu epidemic sweeping across Europe had killed many soldiers who'd survived the fighting, and had now reached Britain. People in London were falling ill, and some were dying.

'I'm thirsty,' Gracie whispered.

'I'll bring a hot drink, luv.'

Polly MacDougal paused in the lobby, trembling with anxiety. What if it was Spanish 'flu? Gracie could die.

She loved her three girls dearly, but somehow Gracie was a special child. Maybe because she'd almost cost Polly's life. Gracie's birth had been complicated and difficult and had ended all hope of giving Joseph the sons he'd longed for.

A man in Joseph's position needed sons. He'd had his heart set on starting a small business one day, but what was the use if there was no son to carry the business forward? Joseph had never reproached her for failing him. He was a wonderful father, devoted to their three pretty daughters. But strangely enough, ever since Grace was tiny, she had helped to fill the gap in Joseph's life because of her genuine interest in mechanical things. It was most unusual in a girl.

As she stood in the darkened lobby, Polly's longing for William Granton's comfort and advice was suddenly overwhelming. But that was over. It had to be, and she had never felt so scared and alone in her life.

Gracie was no better next morning. She lay listless and pale, with bouts of shivering. She couldn't bear to look at her mother and pushed a breakfast tray aside.

'Where does it hurt, dear?' Polly asked.

'In my chest, in my head.'

It was true. Her heart ached, her thoughts hurt.

It was Sunday, but Mum sent Rosie running for the doctor.

Fortunately, Dr Morgan was not one of your superior consultants. He was equally at home in Lady Frances's drawing room or a broken-down slum. His noisy, badly driven old car was a familiar sight all over the East End.

He came clattering cheerfully into the bedroom, Polly hard on his heels.

'Anything I can do, doctor?' she asked anxiously.

'Yes, Polly. Put the kettle on.'

Doctor Morgan sat down beside Gracie. He grinned at her, studied a large rattling pocket watch while taking pulse and temperature, put a hand on her brow, made her say 'Ah' two or three times, then sat back and studied her.

'Tummy upset? Feeling sick?'

'No.'

'Hmm. Tisn't like a healthy little tyke like you to take to bed for no reason. What's wrong, Gracie?'

She stared into shrewd eyes and a sympathetic whiskery face. He was utterly discreet, but she couldn't tell him, because a twisted sense of loyalty stopped her. She squeezed her eyes shut in case the doctor could see the misery inside. Grandma Hawkins had said she was sharp. Oh, how she prayed Grandma was wrong! She didn't want to hurt anyone.

'Just tired,' she mumbled.

The doctor held her hand. His was warm and strong and Gracie's resolve almost weakened, but at that moment Mum came in.

'Kettle's boiled, doctor.'

'Splendid. We'll have a cup of tea. Put plenty sugar in Gracie's. Child's had a severe shock.'

14

'Shock?'

'Classic symptoms,' Dr Morgan nodded. 'Certainly not Spanish 'flu, thank goodness.'

Of course, being young and resilient, Gracie recovered quickly, though she was never quite the same afterwards. Polly noticed a difference, but put it down to her age. The transition from child to woman is difficult at the best of times and somehow her daughter had made the leap much too fast.

Polly caught Gracie watching her sometimes with a look that made her heart lurch. It was not a child's loving look, but cool and appraising like a critical adult's. It was upsetting, but Polly tried not to worry. Anyway she'd enough on her plate just now. Joseph was coming home for Christmas.

Meanwhile, Gracie had quarrelled with Sebastian.

She'd stayed away from the mews purposely because she knew he was on holiday and would be there. To see him would remind her of his father and she could not bear it.

Sebastian had noticed her absence and sought her out as she was coming home from school.

'I've been working on your dad's car, Gracie, polished the chassis and made one or two adjustments to the ignition. She's running sweet as a nut.'

'You've no right to tinker with my father's car!' she said coldly.

'What?' Sebastian was startled. This wasn't the Gracie he knew speaking, the jolly little kid, the good sport.

'I know what you're after,' she went on, narrowing her eyes. 'You're planning to drive my dad's car at Brooklands at crazy speeds. Well, I'll tell him not to let you do it.'

Sebastian studied the girl warily.

He was already wise in the ways of women, at least, young women, and this female was displaying all the

15

symptoms of a jealous sulk. Surprising, he thought, but there you are.

'Listen, Gracie, I'm sorry you're in a huff because I wouldn't dance with you at the party,' he said. 'Maybe it was bad form on my part to go waltzing off with your sister, but Rosie's a jolly good dancer.' Smiling, he deliberately turned on the charm. 'But you're my best girl, Gracie. My one and only girlfriend.'

She shuddered. Somehow the handsome young man reminded her of the two lovers meeting in the darkened mews. An attraction she found disturbing and repellant radiated from him. She felt hot and strange and furious.

She yelled in his face: 'I'm not your girl, Sebastian Granton. I'm not even your friend!' She flounced off, head high.

Sebastian stared after her. He knew what had happened but the suddenness of the event took him by surprise.

Gracie had grown up.

To his surprise, he felt as if he'd lost something he'd valued. He'd been fond of Gracie the child, but he wasn't so sure about Gracie the woman.

Joseph MacDougal came home for Christmas. He came home to a house decorated with paper chains his daughters had draped all round the room, and a Christmas tree Grandma Hawkins had wangled out of Covent Garden. He was greeted with a kiss from his wife and tearful hugs from three daughters, who'd grown into beautiful young ladies during his years of captivity.

Gracie took a keen interest in the reunion, sitting back and watching everything intently. She was reassured. Dad looked different, of course. Prison camp had left its mark and Joseph MacDougal was thin and frail-looking. The stresses of an emotional homecoming brought on an attack of breathless wheezing that was alarming to see. Polly

16

immediately loosened his collar and knelt beside the chair, holding his hand till his breathing eased.

'Blimey, Joe dear, what they done to you?' she said.

'Nothing too bad, Polly, just a whiff of poison gas before I was captured. There's plenty worse off than me.'

'It's bad enough, but you were never a moaner, Joe.'

'Didn't dare! Can't abide camphorated oil or Syrup o' Figs, your favourite remedies, Poll,' he laughed.

Polly ruffled his hair and Gracie rejoiced. She'd prayed that Mum and Dad would fall in love again and it was happening. Of course, Mum was a born nurse and an invalid could count on warm sympathy and her undivided attention.

Maybe Dad's illness was a blessing in disguise. Mum would nurse him back to health and lose interest in Sir William Granton, who was hale and hearty and in no need of nursing – or sympathy either, for that matter, Gracie thought grimly . . .

It was the happiest Christmas Gracie could remember. Dad seemed stronger after two or three night's undisturbed sleep in the spare room and the attacks of breathlessness were not quite so frequent. On the morning of Christmas Eve he announced he felt well enough to take a look at the cars. Polly wasn't sure about that. Her sleeves were rolled up and with Gracie's help she was preparing a Christmas dinner to remember. There was a turkey in the larder ready for roasting tomorrow and a rich plum pudding scattered with lucky threepenny bits, but . . .

'Are you sure you're fit enough, dear?' she asked anxiously.

He smiled. 'Och, Polly, it's only a wee step downstairs. I'm fine.'

'I'll go with you, Dad,' Gracie volunteered. She was sieving cooked chestnuts for stuffing. A weary task.

'No, you don't!' Polly needed the extra pair of hands.

He set off with a smile and a wave, making his way down into the yard. At least he didn't have to go far to work, Gracie thought. But would Dad still work for Sir William, and would Sir William want him to?

'It'll do your father good to get out of the house and back to his beloved motors, poor man,' Polly remarked.

'But he's getting better,' Gracie said. 'He'll soon be well enough to sleep in your room again, won't he?'

'It's rest he needs!' she said abruptly. 'Sieve those chestnuts finer, Gracie. You want to choke us?'

Her mother's tone was irritable, but nothing could dampen Gracie's spirits today.

'It's a magnificent turkey, Mum. Did Grandpa get it cheap from Smithfield market?'

'No. It's Sir William's gift,' Polly answered.

That spoilt the moment, but Gracie recovered. Forcing chestnuts angrily through a fine sieve helped.

The MacDougal girls still clung to family tradition and hung up stockings on Christmas Eve. There was much laughter and excitement on Christmas morning when the bulging stockings were examined. There were apples, sweets and sixpences of course. Dad had socks Mum had knitted and a new pipe, tobacco and pouch. Mum, Rosie and Lily found silk stockings which Dad had bought in Paris, but everyone collapsed with laughter when Gracie held up a full set of spanners.

'Just what I wanted!' she cried delightedly.

Christmas Day could only get better, Gracie thought. She watched Dad kiss Mum under the sprig of mistletoe Gracie had begged from her grandmother's barrow. Mum's pretty fair hair curled loose almost to her shoulders and she looked lovely. Gracie could have cried with happiness.

An aroma of roasting turkey had flavoured the air all morning. The girls helped their mother prepare the feast – roast the potatoes, cook the sprouts, boil the pudding.

18

It was all done with plenty of love and laughter. Gracie decided generously to accept Sir William's turkey as a gift to welcome her father home.

Grandma and Grandpa Hawkins joined the family later on. Grandma was dressed like a duchess in ruby velvet and fringes and they sat down to a table set finely enough to delight any duchess. Lily said grace beautifully.

'Our Lil speaks just like one of them earphone operators,' Grandma said proudly.

'Telephone operators, Gran!' Rosie smiled. 'Earphones are a new hairdo.'

Dad rose to his feet to carve the turkey, perfectly cooked and succulent. Almost a pity to spoil it, he declared laughing. He paused for a moment and looked round them all.

'Maybe now's the time to give you the good news I've kept to myself. I'd a long talk about my job with Sir William. He's taken to driving himself and a chauffeur's not needed, so in compensation he's offered to give me a lease of the mews to open a garage and workshops. I'll be my own boss working in my own business. It's a generous offer.'

Polly had turned pale. 'But Joseph, it takes money to start a business – and we haven't any!'

'That's the beauty of this scheme, love. Sir William has offered to finance the setting up of my business. I said I'd talk it over with you first, of course, but—'

Hearing this, all Gracie's fears for her parents' future happiness resurfaced. She leaped to her feet, toppling the chair.

'No! You can't take that man's money, Dad. You mustn't!'

Her family stared in astonishment. Her father frowned.

'For heaven's sake, lassie, why not?'

She looked at Mum, her glare accusing, then turned again to her father. 'Because it's conscience money, Dad. That's why!'

19

Two

Joseph MacDougal had looked forward to Christmas dinner, his first since the privations of a prison camp. Now his appetite had deserted him. What had Sir William been up to? he wondered.

Joseph had no reason to doubt the man was honest and trustworthy. He was a kind and considerate employer who had supported Joseph's wife and family while he was a prisoner of war. Polly had been allowed to remain rent-free in a tied flat, employed as Lady Frances's maid. She and the girls had been well fed and clothed despite wartime shortages. Now Sir William had offered Joseph capital for a venture which was the fulfilment of his wildest dreams. So what lay behind Gracie's curious statement?

Joseph studied his youngest daughter thoughtfully. Gracie was a sensible girl, not given to making up stories – but of course, he'd been away for three vital years and she wasn't a child any more but a bonnie lass blossoming into a bonnie woman. An image of Sebastian Granton suddenly came into his mind. Might he be the reason for Grace's distress? By heaven, if Master Sebastian was responsible for this he'd be sorry!

Joseph put a hand to his chest. He cursed the whiff of poison gas which had damaged his lungs and troubled his breathing at stressful moments.

'Have the Grantons done something to upset you,

20

Gracie?' he asked her gently. 'Don't be afraid to speak up, lass. Was it Sebastian?'

'Oh no, Dad, not Sebastian . . .'

Gracie hesitated. Her sisters, grandparents, father and mother were waiting for an explanation. But she knew that if she told the truth it would wreck all their lives.

She glanced at her mother, sensing her fear though Polly hadn't said a word. They stared at one another and for a powerful moment both shared the awful dread of exposure.

Oh, Mum, Gracie thought in a sudden burst of maturity, what have you done to our family? Was loving him worth it?

She watched her father press a hand to his chest. The painful wheeze of his breathing sounded loud in the warm room.

'I know Sir William's guilty secret, Dad,' she said deliberately.

'Gracie – please . . . !' she heard her mother whisper.

She paid no attention. 'My friend's mother sent him a white feather, because he's a coward, you see. She says, because he's rich and influential he could dodge call-up and refuse to fight. I expect now you're home, his conscience bothers him and he thinks money can fix anything. You mustn't accept his cowardly money, Dad!'

Joseph smiled his relief. The lass had been listening to gossip, that's all!

'Gracie dear, that's nonsense. Sir William was working for the War Office and couldn't join up even if he wanted to.'

Rosie and Lily laughed and Joseph beamed around the festive table.

'Well, our Gracie picked up the wrong end o' the stick, but it's easily done. There were plenty silly women who handed out white feathers to innocent men. Maybe Sir

William didn't fight in the trenches but he's been a good friend to our family and I'll accept his offer.'

'Will you make loads of money in your garage, Dad?' Lily asked.

'I wouldn't be surprised, once Gracie gets busy with her new spanners,' he joked. He glanced at his wife, realizing she'd been unusually quiet. 'What d'you say, Polly?'

'I say the dinner's growing cold, my dear,' she answered quietly. Her gaze was fixed steadily upon Gracie, he noticed, who was studiously avoiding her mother's eyes. The almost palpable tension between the two bothered Joseph as he carved the turkey. Another of William Granton's generous gifts, as it happened!

Conscience money? Joseph frowned. Maybe there *was* a grain of truth in Gracie's accusation after all . . .

Afterwards they played traditional family games ending with charades, Grace's favourite. Usually she loved this happy, carefree time, and this year should have been happiest of all now Dad was home. But on that cold Wednesday evening with the parlour fire casting a cosy glow and gaslight reflecting golden gleams from shining brasses, fun and laughter seemed inappropriate.

Grandma Hawkins' unerring instinct told her that something was wrong. She had been studying Gracie quietly since the scene at dinner and what she saw worried her.

'Let's have a sing-song round the old joanna,' she suggested cheerfully. She prodded Grandpa. 'C'mon Bert, you play by ear, don't you?'

'No, ma'am, not by 'ere, usually in 'ammersmith.' He grinned.

'Oh, get away with you, you old joker!' Laughing, she gave him a playful shove towards the piano stool.

Gracie watched them. Why couldn't Mum and Dad be like these two dear old souls, loving and faithful to the end

22

of their days? Grandpa ran his fingers effortlessly over the keys. Softly and faultlessly he began to play . . .

'Oh, come all ye faithful . . .'

Gracie bowed her head and let the tears flow. Fortunately nobody noticed.

Except her mother.

Polly came to Gracie's room after Gran and Grandpa had driven off in his old Austin van, a familiar sight at Covent Garden. Joseph was seated by the parlour fire relaxing, while Rosie and Lily were in the kitchen drinking cocoa and altering the hemline of a dress in line with fashion, which was edging daringly upwards.

Gracie had gone to bed early pleading a slight headache, though really she only wanted to be alone for a while. She was brushing her hair in front of the mirror when her mother tapped and came in. Gracie went on counting brushstrokes:

'Twenty . . . twenty one . . .'

'Why did you lie, Gracie?' Polly sat on the bed and looked at her.

'I *did* have a headache. It's gone now.'

'I meant earlier on. You lied to Dad about Sir William.'

'Some of it was true.'

'But the rest wasn't. You knew perfectly well he was in a reserved occupation. I told you so myself. So why did you lie?'

Gracie flung down the hairbrush.

'Because the truth is too cruel and awful for Dad to know. I would never tell him you loved someone else. Neither must you!'

'Oh, my dear! How did you find out?' Polly whispered.

'I left the Drill Hall early on the night of the Armistice dance, remember? I went into the workshop and sat in Dad's car. I heard you and Sir William talking, I heard every single word.'

'Gracie dear, listen to me . . .' Polly said desperately. 'I didn't know for months if your father was dead or alive. I had to seem hopeful and cheery for your sakes, but how could I be cheery when I saw long casualty lists? As time passed I gave up hope. That was a dreadful time and William was kind. He understands sorrow, you see. He knows Lady Frances will never get better.'

'That poor lady! Ohh . . . how could you?'

'One day you'll understand,' Polly sighed, '—when you fall in love yourself, my dear.'

'No!' She whirled round to face her mother. 'I never will. I won't let it happen. You've ruined it for me.'

'Don't put another burden on my conscience, Gracie, for I couldn't stand it!' Polly cried angrily. 'I swear it's over. Finished.'

'No, it isn't,' Gracie said. 'I've seen the way he looks at you. How long do you think it'll be before Dad notices?'

Rosie MacDougal stamped her feet on the slushy pavement, hobnailed boots sending trampled snow flying into the gutter. It was no joke working on the barrows in this weather. She wished the snow would fall in earnest and drive Uncle Sid Hawkins indoors to a stance in the shopping arcade. More expensive, but warmer. Bundled-up as she was with jerseys, coats and mufflers till only eyes and red nose showed, Rosie still shivered. Business was slack that morning. Funny thing, she thought, you always feel warm when business is booming.

'Onions big as bunions, only tuppence a pound!' she yelled.

Uncle Sid had a customer round the other side. 'Cauliflowers 'ere, lady! We got cauliflower ears in our family, y'know. Me dad was an 'eavyweight boxer.'

Rosie giggled. Sid's sales patter was a good laugh. She'd

learned a lot from her uncle and the other traders. There
was an art in laying out flowers, fruit and veg to attract
customers. People like to prod the produce and sneak a
grape or two on the sly, Sid said. You'll never stop 'em,
bless their little hearts, so make sure it's the produce they
squeeze and the bunch of grapes they pinch from that you
pops in their bag, girl.

'Cauliflowers 'ere!' she bellowed merrily.

There was a chuckle behind her and she whipped round
hoping for a sale, only to be confronted by her worst
nightmare.

'Oh, my giddy aunt! Sebastian Granton!'

'It can't be Rosie MacDougal?' He was astonished.

'Well, it's not the bloomin' *Mona Lisa*,' Rosie said
gloomily.

'What on earth are you doing here?' He laughed.

'This is what I do. I work the barrows.'

'When you're not dancing the turkey-trot?'

'I don't go dancing. Me mum won't let me.'

'Freedom is at hand. Women have the vote.'

'Only old women over thirty.'

'Your day will come.' He glanced at vegetables dis-
played on the barrow. 'You have cauliflowers 'ere, I
believe.'

'Yes.' She scowled.

'I'll have one, please.'

He whistled when she told him the price. 'That's dear!'

'They're scarce. It's winter, hadn't you noticed in your
big warm 'ouse?'

'Funny, your wee sister Grace doesn't like me either,
Rosie.' He laughed as he paid up. 'I wish somebody would
explain what I've done to upset the MacDougals.' He raised
his cap and went on his way.

Her uncle appeared from behind the barrow. 'Who's
the toff?'

25

'Young Master Granton. Wanted to know if we'd cauli-flowers 'ere.'

'Did you give 'im one?'

'Just about.'

She was puzzling over Gracie giving Sebastian the cold shoulder. They'd been thick as thieves in younger days. As a matter of fact it was odd how drastically Gracie's sunny outlook had changed recently, now she came to think about it.

'May as well get it orf me chest, Rosie.' Sid coughed bashfully. 'I'm getting spliced at last.'

'You choosy old bachelor, you!' She hugged him delightedly. 'Who's the lucky lady?'

'Respectable widow-woman name of Gladys Barlow. She put in a standing order for parsnips an' green beans last summer an' we been courting ever since. I popped the question last weekend, along with a pound of sprouts an' a winter cabbage.'

'And the wise woman snapped you up before somebody else did. Good for her!'

'Don' know about that, Rosie.' He turned beetroot-red. 'Gladys has a nice comfy 'ouse an' a bright young lad who could be 'andy on the barrows.'

'When's the wedding?'

'Sometime in February. Thought a winter wedding would cheer folks up.'

She slipped an arm through his.

'Remember to tell Mrs Barlow you have three lovely nieces ready and waiting to be bridesmaids, dear Uncle Sid.'

Gracie was glad of the hustle and bustle preparing for her uncle's wedding. The announcement had caused consider-able stir in the neighbourhood since everyone had assumed Sid was a confirmed bachelor.

Sid's wife-to-be accepted the offer of bridesmaids and generously supplied Polly with cash to buy dress material, any colour, providing it toned with dove-grey.

They settled upon plum-red velvet, bright and cheerful for a chilly February and practical for afterwards. Polly then sought permission to use the sewing machine in the dressmaker's room in the Granton's mansion. She intended making the bridesmaids' dresses in the evening after work, which roused Gracie's suspicions. Was her mother still meeting Sir William?

'I'll help with the sewing when I come home from school,' she declared.

Polly opened her mouth to protest, then caught her daughter's eye and sighed. 'Oh, very well!'

So every evening Gracie tacked and hemmed and guarded her mother. Her schoolwork suffered seriously in consequence, but keeping Sir William Granton and her mother apart seemed to Gracie a worthwhile cause. At last Rosie and Lily's dresses were finished and only the disputed length of Gracie's skirt remained to be fixed.

Polly pinned the hem then sat back on her heels.

'No matter what you say, Gracie, that's too short. Go into the corridor and see for yourself. There's a full-length mirror at the end.'

The big house was deathly quiet as Gracie stepped into the corridor. The ornate ceilings were so high above her head it was like being in church and you couldn't hear a footfall on the thick carpets. It was strange to think that Sebastian had grown up here.

Gracie shivered, pitying a little boy cloistered in this lonely house that should have echoed to the fun and laughter of a large family. No wonder he'd escaped to the mews whenever he could, to car engines, oil and petrol, not to mention the company of an understanding man and a chattering little girl.

The mirror was set in the wall at the end of the lobby, where it widened out with bedroom doors on either side. Gracie watched herself walking towards the reflection under the electric wall sconces. The dress was simply cut and her tall, slender figure showed the embroidered velvet to advantage. The skirt was shorter than she normally wore, but she definitely didn't want it lengthened. Even with black woollen stockings and sensible school shoes her ankles and calves were slim and elegant.

She had a heady sense of freedom, as if she might dance the polka if only Sebastian should appear.

'Very pretty,' a voice said.

Gracie whirled round. The door to Lady Frances's suite of rooms stood wide open and she found herself facing the invalid lady.

'Thank you, ma'am.' She bobbed an awkward curtsey. She'd seen Lady Frances many times of course, but always at a distance, in a coach or landau or seated in the rose garden in summertime. She hadn't realized how beautiful she was.

Mum was healthily pretty and lively, but Lady Granton's looks were fragile, angelic and quite breathtaking.

'Red is your colour.' Lady Frances smiled. 'It suits you.'

'My mother says the dress is too short. What do you think?' Gracie asked shyly. This was a real lady. She would know.

'No, it's not too short.' She put her head to one side. 'It's young and modern and you have very nice ankles. Why not show them off?'

'I *do* feel freer in short skirts, ma'am, I could dance the polka!' she admitted delightedly.

A shadow passed over Lady Frances's face.

'Then you should wear them and keep dancing!' she said firmly. 'One never knows what lies ahead.'

Grace guessed that she was thinking about the illness that was slowly crippling her limbs and keeping her a helpless invalid in this silent house. But the lady did not know she'd been betrayed by people she loved and trusted. Gracie's knowledge was harder to bear now they'd met.

'Oh, ma'am, I'm so sorry you're ill,' she said tearfully.

Lady Frances looked at her for a long moment with an expression Gracie couldn't fathom.

'You're Sebastian's friend Gracie MacDougal, aren't you?' she said presently. 'My son tells me you're a very clever mechanic.'

'I suppose so, but there's no future in engineering for a woman, ma'am.'

'Why not?'

'Your hands get dirty.'

'That's a pathetic excuse, Gracie MacDougal. Hands can be washed!' the lady declared severely.

'I . . . I suppose so.' Gracie would have continued the argument but the invalid was obviously growing tired. 'Can I help you back to bed, ma'am?' she asked.

'No, dear, you might ask your mother to come.' She patted Gracie's cheek. 'Stay free, Gracie MacDougal. Remember you can be anything you want to be.'

'Yes, ma'am, I'll remember.'

As she ran to fetch her mother, Grace was aware this meeting with Frances Granton was memorable, but at that moment she could hardly be expected to know how greatly the brief encounter would influence her future . . .

Sidney and Gladys, the bride-to-be, had prepared a discreet guest list and sent out invitations, but they needn't have bothered. The church was packed to the doors and at the reception afterwards in the Eight Bells there was barely enough room for a knees-up.

Gracie was relieved to find plenty of short skirts on

bright young things quite a bit older than herself. Young girls danced with youths who had escaped the war, and these youngsters danced as people had never danced before – madly, exuberantly and, their elders declared in shocked tones, shamelessly.

Rosie loved the new dances that had crept in from America with American soldiers stationed in England in the latter part of the war. Toes tapping, she stood beside a wonderful array of food laid out in the supper room and searched the dance floor hopefully for Sebastian Granton.

Why on earth he should be at her Uncle Sid's wedding she couldn't imagine, but everyone else in the district was, so why not?

'Looking for a partner, luv?' A cheeky young fellow with brilliantined hair appeared at her elbow.

'No, thanks.'

'Pity. Let me introduce meself. I'm your cousin Edwin.'

'I know my cousins. You're not one of 'em.'

'I'm the newest. Your uncle just married my ma.'

'Oh, that one!' Rosie was not delighted to meet a potential rival.

'Uncle Sid's giving you a job on the barrow, isn't he?'

'Start next week on the straight and narrow,' he nodded. Then paused as the band changed to a completely new tempo. 'They're playing the tango. Care to try it out?'

Rosie hesitated, but her foot was already tapping to a compulsive rhythm. The tango was new and rather daring and the floor had cleared so the older generation could settle back and watch youngsters making fools of themselves.

Rosie couldn't resist it. She'd have preferred Sebastian but could make do with Edwin.

'Don't mind if I do,' she agreed graciously.

He grabbed her hand and they swept out on to the dance floor, arms extended, heels clicking.

*   *   *

30

Gracie's schoolwork had always been excellent, second in reading, writing and English grammar, top in arithmetic. But as the year 1919 progressed towards important examinations in May, her marks went steadily downhill.

Unfortunately nobody realized the strain she was under. At home she kept constant watch upon both her parents, worrying night and day that her father would discover her mother's secret, or that her mother would take up with Sir William again. How could Gracie possibly concentrate on lessons with all that intrigue preying on her mind?

Sending for Gracie after the exam papers had been marked, the head teacher looked at her bright pupil in despair. What on earth had come over the girl?

'I can hardly find words to tell you how disappointed I am with your results, Grace,' she said. 'I was confident you'd win a scholarship to grammar school, but that's out of the question with poor marks like these.'

'I'm very sorry, Miss.' Gracie hung her head.

'So am I, Grace. Our country needs clever young women. You'll be leaving us at the end of term now, I'm afraid.'

The head sighed. It saddened her when a clever girl started paying more attention to attracting boys than studying books. She'd seen it happen many times when girls reached the critical age of fourteen, but in Gracie MacDougal's case it really was a tragedy.

If Gracie's parents were disappointed by the news she'd failed her exams, they hid it well that evening. Polly took the practical view.

'I don't deny a good education's useful, Gracie luv, but earning cash pays the groceries!' She continued with the ironing. 'That's more use to us in my book.'

'Look at me for instance, Gracie,' Lily added comfortingly. 'I started work cleaning phones in the telephone exchange and now I've been promoted to probationer switchboard operator, earning twelve and six a week.'

Rosie was reading the *Dancing Times*. She glanced up. 'And I'd earn a blooming sight more if I didn't have to split the profits with cousin Edwin!'

'Well, I don't know what I'll do,' Gracie said gloomily.

She had always intended to win a bursary place to grammar school, then after that – who knows? Maybe even a course in engineering. She'd planned to help her father design cars. She could see a great future ahead for the motor car – but not for herself, alas. She was a failure, at fourteen!

Polly folded Joseph's newly ironed shirt.

'You could go into service with the Grantons, Gracie. I could speak up for you. It'd be good training for running your own household one day, luv.'

The idea absolutely appalled her.

'I suppose I could keep an eye on you if I was the Grantons' skivvy, Mum, that's the only advantage I can see,' she retorted.

Polly gave her daughter a furious glance. Joseph was in the room. What would he make of that remark?

'Somehow I can't see our Gracie as a skivvy, Poll.' He frowned. 'I have a better plan. Why shouldn't Gracie work in the garage with me? I could only pay pocket money, but it'd save paying wages till I find my feet, then I'll see Gracie doesn't lose out.'

'It's dirty work, Joseph.' Polly wasn't enthusiastic. 'I should know, scrubbing your bloomin' filthy overalls!'

'The lass needn't dirty her hands,' Joseph argued. 'There's accounts and bookkeeping to be done and plenty other work suitable for a young lady.' He turned to his daughter. 'What d'you say, Gracie?'

The future suddenly looked brighter.

'I say, yes, please, Dad!'

Polly thudded the flat iron on to damp linen with an angry sizzle. She didn't like the plan but could think of no way to stop it. She had an uneasy premonition that this arrangement would cause everyone a great deal of grief.

The following year was one of the happiest Gracie had ever known, though there were poignant moments. Working closely with her father, she saw his limitations at first hand. She could only begin to imagine how much he had suffered as a prisoner of war. Though officially Gracie's job was in the office, bookkeeping, more than once she quickly and efficiently repaired a faulty transmission or changed spark plugs for impatient customers while her father rested and wheezed breathlessly.

Sebastian turned up at odd times. He was attending the London School of Economics to gain a degree in business studies before entering his father's office, but his first love was still the motor car.

Gracie was friendly enough with Sebastian now, but never forgot he was a Granton and a younger version of his treacherous father. She vowed never to trust him.

He was a clever engineer though, and had suggested worthwhile improvements to the two-seater racing car which remained Joseph's spare time hobby and Gracie's delight. The compact little racer remained idle in the garage although its engine had been tuned to perfection by the pair of them. Then one Friday in September when Gracie and Sebastian were arguing over various methods of speedy tyre change – essential on the race circuit, Sebastian maintained – her father interrupted.

'Why don't we test drive this baby at Brooklands then?'

'Don't we need permission?'

'We have it. There's a customer interested in a sale if it can pass muster on the track and he's fixed up a trial run for us. You'll have to drive, Sebastian. I'm not up to it.'

'You'll take the mechanic's seat, though?' Sebastian asked.

'No. I'll wait in the pit.'

'Oh, but I must have a mechanic in case anything goes wrong out on the track, Joe.' Sebastian frowned.

'What about me?' Gracie said.

She was excited. If the car performed well and the rich customer bought it, that could be the start of a profitable sideline. Motor racing was a rich man's sport. She held her breath, waiting for her father's reply.

Joseph was doubtful. He wasn't keen to see his bonnie daughter sitting in the mechanic's seat. A dirty, dangerous job! On the other hand, if Gracie was aboard, young Granton wouldn't dare take risks.

'Very well, Gracie,' he agreed reluctantly. He turned to the young man. 'I'm trusting you to take care of her, Sebastian.'

'Don't worry, I will!' he promised delightedly. He put an arm across Gracie's shoulders in a friendly gesture. She shrugged it off and glared.

Sebastian was hurt. What on earth had he done to offend her now?

Gracie could pass for a youth when dressed in her father's overalls, hair hidden under a black beret. When they arrived at the racetrack a few weeks later nobody gave the young lass a second glance. All those present were far too interested in Joseph's car as he drove it off the trailer.

There was no racing planned that day, only test drives and practice sessions, and when their turn came, Gracie nervously fitted on racing goggles and took her place in the mechanic's seat next to Sebastian.

'Don't look so petrified.' He smiled. 'A mechanic should have confidence in his driver and a driver should have faith in his mechanic. No loose hub nuts and the engine in first-class order.'

'And you have faith in me?'

'We have faith in one another, don't we, Gracie?' He was serious for once, turning to look at her meaningfully.

'Just keep your eyes on the rev counter, Sebastian,' she said.

He scowled and started the engine.

'OK. We'll try to average seventy miles an hour.'

'That's too fast—!'

But they were off, the wind whipping dust in her face, the tyres kicking sand from the track.

'Flat out on the straight, Gracie. What a delight!' he yelled.

'Too fast, Sebastian . . . !' she screamed, gripping the sides.

Fortunately her safety-conscious father had fitted lap belts.

'Don't worry, girl!' Sebastian laughed. He shouted above engine noise and the racket of the slip-stream: 'Women don't understand speed. When a woman drives she must have a boring destination in mind – shopping, visiting friends, picnics!'

'Cheek!' she yelled. 'Sebastian, look out! The bend.'

He braked, then accelerated smoothly into the bend and speeded flat out along the straight. She squealed, he grinned.

'Sorry, old girl. Can't learn to race going slow, you know!'

She said no more, clinging grimly to the seat and keeping an eye on the rev counter as it climbed higher. When they'd completed the gruelling test laps, Sebastian gradually slowed down and guided the car into the service pit.

Her father was waiting for them on the counter. Joseph's lips twitched when he saw his daughter's oil-blackened face. Sebastian's wasn't much better.

'Well done, you two!' he called. 'The car's performance

impressed our customer. I think we may have sold our first MacDougal!'

Sebastian's chest swelled with pride, and yet he felt curiously humbled by the difficulty of the drive. He knew he had courage, but driving on the race circuit required exceptional skill. He had plenty to learn if this was what he wanted to do.

Gracie had taken off the goggles protecting her eyes, leaving two big clownish areas of white on a blackened face. It looked comical, but Sebastian didn't feel like laughing.

There was something heroic about the girl. She'd been scared stiff at times during their hair-raising drive, but hadn't made a song and dance like other girls he knew.

He smiled and pulled a small box from the pocket of his leather jerkin.

'Here, Gracie. Present for the mechanic.'

She took it curiously and opened the lid.

'Oh!' she gasped.

It was a little gilt motor car, perfect in every detail and mounted as a brooch. It was so beautiful and such a thoughtful gift, Gracie forgot antagonism and slipped into their old, easy ways.

'Oh, Sebastian, thank you. It's beautiful. I'll treasure it for ever and ever, I promise!'

Joseph had climbed down into the pit and was standing beside them. She let her father see the brooch, eyes shining.

'Dad, look what Sebastian gave me. See how brightly the little glass headlamps shine!'

Joseph studied the rich young man's gift in silence, then stared hard at Sebastian.

'Glass?'

Sebastian looked away, drumming his fingertips on the steering wheel. Joseph MacDougal could recognize gold, diamonds and rubies when he saw them. He didn't like this development. He didn't like it at all. He found it awkward to handle.

He'd been pleased to see that his blossoming young daughter kept young Master Sebastian firmly in his place – at arm's length. She didn't seem to care for the young rascal and was quite indifferent to his persuasive charm.

But of course indifference can be a powerful challenge to a man accustomed to have young ladies fighting one another for his attention.

Joseph considered ordering his daughter to return the expensive gift but feared that would only make matters worse. Gracie had no idea of its value and would probably soon tire of the bauble and consign it carelessly to the back of a drawer.

There was a more subtle way of dealing with this situation!

'I must say that's a fine memento of the time you spent as your dad's mechanic, Gracie.' He smiled jovially. 'I was meaning to tell you it was time you moved on.'

'What d'you mean, move on?' She stared in dismay at her father.

'Find a more congenial job for you. There's no future in my garage for a girl, Gracie. Look at the mess you're in! Your bonnie face is filthy.'

'But you need me!' she cried in panic. 'If you sack me you'll have to find someone else and pay him wages!'

'I can afford to if I sell this car. I might have orders for more after today's showing. Anyway, Gracie, I've had someone in mind for a wee while, a young lad I knew in prison camp. He needs the job more than you do, you know.'

Gracie looked helplessly to Sebastian for support. It was not forthcoming.

Sebastian was wise in the ways of fathers protecting their

precious daughters. He had realized the moment he met Joseph's cold gaze that the specially commissioned little jewel from a high-class jeweller was a serious mistake.

Gracie turned to her father on the verge of tears. 'You said I was a first-class mechanic. You said I was one of the best you'd ever known.'

'You are, Gracie,' he said gently. 'But it's no job for a woman and your mother's never been happy about it. She would've fainted if she'd seen the risks you took today driving with Sebastian.'

'No, she wouldn't!' Her control snapped. 'You don't know her, Dad. She lives dangerously every day she's with the Grantons!'

'What are you saying, Grace?' He stared in astonishment. 'What do you mean?'

Gracie glared at her father. All right, I'll tell him about Mum and Sir William, she thought angrily. Why should I spare his feelings? He doesn't care tuppence about mine.

But before she could utter a word Sebastian intervened angrily. 'Well, I'm disappointed in you, Gracie MacDougal!' he cried resentfully. 'I know what people are saying, but I never dreamt that you of all people would spread it around!'

Gracie stared open-mouthed. Had he known about Mum and his father all this time and never said a cheep?

'I never told anyone, Sebastian, honest. It was too hurtful. Your poor mother—'

'Yes, my poor mother!' he said. 'There's no truth in the rumour she has T.B. and should be put in a sanitorium. Her illness is not infectious and your mother's in no danger. So will you kindly shut up and stop spreading malicious gossip?'

'I agree.' Her father frowned at her. 'I know you're upset at the moment, Gracie, but that's no reason to tell tales that could harm Lady Frances and alarm your mother. That doesn't solve anything, my dear.'

Gracie looked at the two men in her life in despair. She knew only too well that the truth can be twisted to mean whatever you want to believe.

She sighed despondently. Why fight against the inevitable outcome? Her father had made up his mind, and no matter what he decided about her future, she must obey.

She remembered Lady Granton's stirring words.

'You can be anything you want to be, Grace MacDougal!' If only that were true.

Three

W ithin the next week Joseph MacDougal told Gracie that he'd managed to find her a job in Ramptons' factory. But . . .

'Bicycles?' she cried in dismay.

'Why not? It's a perfect solution, Gracie. A lass with your ability will have no difficulty assembling bicycles, and it's a largely female workforce so you'll make plenty of friends.'

'If I don't die of boredom first. All those fiddly bits!'

'A bicycle is a miracle of engineering, my girl! It's the only vehicle on the road driven by manpower alone. You should be proud.'

'Well, I'm not,' she said gloomily.

She studied the empty space in the workshop where the prototype 'MacDougal's Luck' used to stand. Their customer had bought the car for a staggering sum and already Joseph and Sebastian had their heads together designing a faster, much improved model. Gracie longed to join them. Not that racing interested her, but she could see that improvements developed on the racetrack could be adapted to improve performance on the road. There was so much she wanted to learn about engineering techniques. And what did her father have in mind for her future?

Bloomin' bicycles!

Everyone in the Granton area knew Ramptons, a huge square brick building on the fringe of the East End. There

was a smartly painted red sign across the front with a large
iron replica of a penny-farthing bicycle hung above. The
window frames were painted white and Gracie had to admit
the place looked smart and prosperous as she walked in on
her first day through red gates leading to the factory yard.
The yard was choc-a-bloc with workers' bikes.

'You new?' one woman asked, dismounting and stacking
her machine with the rest. 'You'll have to get a bike, luv.
It's expected.'

Gracie smiled politely. She'd wait and see first.

Strangely enough, after a day or two she found the
work interesting. As her father had said, the bicycle was
a miracle of miniature engineering and there was much
to be learned from its construction. She had been put
to work helping Connie Dougan. Connie was a middle-
aged operative assembling the head tubes of triangular
bicycle frames which had been tailored, brazed, aligned
and painted by men working in the sultry heat of the
welding shop. Gracie's job was fitting ball bearings into
a circular retainer and handing Connie the retainers, dust
seals and locknut washers when required. Ball bearings
were fiddly to handle and easily scattered, but otherwise
it was not demanding work. Connie worked, while filling
Gracie in on factory gossip.

'There's Mr Rampton Senior, the boss, Gracie. He's
elderly and a proper gentleman, keeps an eye on the books
and hardly ever stirs from his office. His lumbago's bad,
poor soul. Then there's young Mr Rampton, who keeps an
eye on assembly line and shop floor. He's a real charmer.
New girls go potty about young Mr Rampton.'

'Well, don't worry about me, Connie, 'cause I won't!'
Gracie said.

Connie gave her a quick approving glance. 'Good for
you!' she said, vigorously tightening a locknut.

Gracie hadn't been working on the assembly line for

more than a fortnight before she saw room for improvement. She aired her views with Connie.

'Why don't frame workers change places with stem workers so that girls assembling chain rings, brakes and pedal cranks can reach the components store directly instead of making an awkward detour?'

'Maybe 'cause nobody thought of it, luv. Why not suggest that to the boss? You could write down your brainwave and pop it in the suggestion box. If it isn't too daft they might consider it. If it saves time and money you could get a two bob bonus in your wage packet – if you're lucky.'

Greatly excited by the project, Gracie spent time that evening drawing a detailed plan reassembling the assembly line and next day diffidently dropped the result into the suggestion box. Nothing happened right away, but a few days later a shadow fell across Gracie's work station and she looked up to find young Mr Rampton standing smiling.

He was a charmer all right, a tall dark, film-star type a little older than Sebastian and even more handsome. Why do I use Sebastian Granton as a yardstick? Gracie thought with a flash of annoyance.

Young Mr Rampton's friendly smile was heart-stopping. 'Congratulations, Miss MacDougal, Mr Rampton Senior was most impressed by the way you presented your ideas. Well done indeed!'

'Th-thank you very much, sir,' she stammered, eyes like stars. How strange if working for Ramptons turned out to be the pathway to her ambitions! If Mr Rampton Senior was impressed he might send her to college to study, or at least arrange for her to attend night school. The young man smiled warmly and moved on.

Connie giggled knowingly. 'Told you so! Young Mr Rampton always keeps an eye on talent in the assembly line!'

Gracie had her coat and hat on after work and was almost out the door behind Connie, unfurling her brolly against a sudden downpour of rain when he waylaid her.

'Miss MacDougal, could you spare a moment?' young Mr Rampton called.

Connie glanced over her shoulder. ''Ere, Gracie . . . !'

She barely heard her. Excitedly, she followed the tall young man upstairs to his office. Maybe they'd decided to adopt her plan!

'Shut the door,' he said.

She obeyed and he smiled. 'Now, Miss MacDougal. What's this about the assembly line?'

'Well, sir, I can see the girls waste time getting across to the store room when they're running short of components, and I thought—'

He broke in, smiling. 'Oh, come off it, Gracie! I saw through the subterfuge, you know!'

'Subterfuge?'

'You can't tell me pretty girls are interested in assembly lines! You want to catch my eye, don't you? Maybe you hope for a little flirtation with the boss?'

'No, I certainly do not!'

'Of course you do! Bright little sparkler like you.' He took a step nearer.

She backed away, cold with anger. 'You've too high an opinion of yourself, Mr Rampton!'

He followed, laughing. 'I know, and it's well-founded. Girls fall for me, Gracie. I can pick and choose and I've chosen you. You should be flattered, darling.'

He was too close for comfort. In a moment he would be between Gracie and all hope of escape. She raised the brolly and hit him hard. He sprang back, yelling. 'Ow, you wicked little vixen!'

She wrenched open the door and clattered downstairs. He shouted after her, 'Don't bother to come back. You're sacked, Grace MacDougal, and I'll tell anyone who asks, you were absolutely useless.'

Connie was waiting anxiously outside in the rain. She took one look at the distressed girl and took her in her arms. 'Gracie, luv, I should've warned you the man has a bad reputation, but you swore you wouldn't be taken in. What happened, dearie?'

She raised a tear-stained face. 'I hit him with my brolly.'

'Good for you, luv!' She beamed her satisfaction. 'That'll make him think twice next poor girl he fancies!'

Gracie dried her eyes and squared her shoulders. Now she'd got over the shock she felt wonderful, fully in command.

She laughed. 'He gave me the sack, Connie, and am I glad!'

She linked arms with her friend and walked out, head held high.

But her father and mother weren't so pleased. 'Sacked?' her father groaned. 'I can't understand it, Gracie. What did you do?'

'Mr Rampton said I was useless.'

Not for the world would she tell them she'd been taken in by a handsome rascal.

Her father snorted. 'I can't believe that! Unless . . .' He studied his young daughter suspiciously. 'Did you make a mess of that job deliberately so's I'd take you back?'

'Course not! I told them how to run the assembly line. It was a mess.'

His brow cleared. 'Ah, well, no wonder they sacked you! What else did you expect for your cheek, Miss Know-it-all?'

Polly sighed. 'That's all very well, Joseph, but what's she to do now? Everyone in this family has to earn their keep till the garage gets on its feet. Ramptons won't give a glowing reference. Will they, Gracie?'

She almost laughed. 'Definitely not.'

'Very well then,' her father sighed. 'I'll take you back till we decide what's to be done with you, Gracie. The new mechanic's working his notice and won't start till the beginning of the month so I could do with a hand, though Sebastian's been helpful. You'll only get pocket money, mind.'

She smiled radiantly. 'That suits me!'

Lady Frances was having a bad turn. The bell rang that night and Polly was called out. The sound wakened Gracie with a start, afraid for Lady Frances and afraid that her mother and Sir William might find themselves alone together at night. The poor lady's health had improved for a long spell and the night-time bell had not summoned Polly for months. Gracie did not consider the chances of a daytime meeting quite so hazardous, since there was plenty staff around and William Granton was usually safely out of the way at the office. She had been lulled into a false sense of security, but the hours of darkness presented opportunities . . .

Rosie and Lily stirred restlessly and grumbled, then went back to sleep, but Gracie lay sleepless. There was nothing she could do to prevent a meeting. She couldn't rush across to the big house and barge in. She could only lie in bed imagining the worst.

Polly and William Granton sat side by side at his wife's bedside. It was the closest they'd been since Joseph came home and it played havoc with the emotions.

Polly had dispensed Frances's medication and watched it take effect. Her lady's breathing eased and she'd closed her eyes and lay peacefully quiet. William held his wife's hand, but glanced at Polly and risked a whisper.

45

'I've missed you, Polly.'

'Shh, William!' She glanced in terror at the sleeping woman.

'She's drugged. She can't hear us, poor darling.' He stared sadly at his wife. 'I love her, you know, Polly. I wouldn't hurt her for the world. If Frances had kept well, if we'd had the large family we always planned, then—'

'You'd never have looked my way,' Polly said.

'I might've looked, but I would never have strayed.' He smiled.

'I love you,' she told him simply. 'You're not perfect and neither am I, while your dear lady . . .' She looked fondly at her mistress. 'Well, she deserves loyalty. That's why I'm glad Joseph came home and it had to end. I can look my lady in the eye without hating meself now.'

'Are you happy, Polly?' His face was shadowed. 'Is Joseph happy?'

'I don't know. We don't speak much about such things. He's happy when he's in the garage. That's a wonderful thing you did for him, William!'

'Not for him. For you! If Granton's goes under, you and Joseph will be all right. I've made sure of that. It's the least I can do for you, Polly my love.'

Dimmed lamps cast deep shadows in the beautiful bedroom but a muffled sob from Polly betrayed emotion.

'Are you crying?' he whispered.

'Course I am! What you said would make a bloomin' statue cry!' She took out a hanky and dabbed her eyes. 'You'd better get some sleep, William, or Granton's really will go bust tomorrow. I'll sit with my lady.'

'Thanks, Polly, I *am* tired out,' he said yawning.

Business was difficult these days. The value of shares had fallen sharply and the country showed signs of slipping into recession. He needed to keep a steady nerve.

William stood up and kissed his wife's cheek before kissing Polly tenderly.

'I don't know if I'm foolish or fortunate to be in love with two wonderful women.'

'Bit of both, I'd say, luv.' She smiled fondly.

When he'd gone to his room, Polly settled down to keep vigil till morning. Lady Frances stirred restlessly, and breathed her husband's name.

'Ahh . . . William!'

'Hush, ma'am.' Polly soothed her. 'He's tired, He's sleeping.'

Frances Granton turned her face away from dim light into shadow, so that Polly MacDougal wouldn't see the tears . . .

Lily MacDougal was now a fully fledged telephone operator. She took her place confidently in a roomful of smart young women and worked on a switchboard that would seem daunting to most. Lily was bright and quick with perfect diction. She was happy at her work and the corners of her pretty mouth lifted in a smile. You could hear the brightness of her sunny smile reflected in her voice.

'Operator. Can I help you?' she said that springlike morning.

On the end of the line a male voice answered. 'I need to make a long-distance call to Manchester, miss, but I can't remember the lady's number.'

It was a pleasant voice, slow, deep and friendly. It made Lily smile. 'Shall I put you through to Directory Enquiries, sir? They could tell you.'

'Oh, is that what one does? I'm not familiar with telephones, you see, or directories either.'

'They do take some getting used to, sir.'

She was about to plug him in to Enquiries when he

said softly: 'Her voice was ever gentle, sweet and low, an excellent thing in woman.'

'I beg your pardon?'

'A quotation from Shakespeare. You have a beautiful voice.'

She was speechless. Fortunately the man couldn't see her blushes.

'Are you still there? If I've embarrassed you I do apologize.'

'No. It was a lovely compliment. Thank you.' Hastily, she put him through to Enquiries.

Operators were not encouraged to chat with callers – it was severely frowned upon. She felt quite breathless after the strange encounter. A beautiful voice! She was used to compliments because of her looks but this was the nicest she'd ever had, from somebody who didn't even know what she looked like.

She'd almost forgotten the incident when the familiar voice came on again some days later: 'Long distance to Manchester!'

'What number are you calling, sir?'

'Why, it's the girl with the lovely voice! You'll be pleased to hear I've committed the lady's number to memory this time.'

'Lucky lady,' Lily said smiling as he reeled it off. She prepared to make the connection.

'Wait a minute! Please, would you tell me your name?'

She hesitated. This was strictly taboo, but he did sound nice!

'It's Lily,' she admitted shyly.

'Lily!' The name came ringing along the line like a peal of bells. 'I knew it would be a beautiful name!'

'Trying to connect you,' she said hurriedly. 'Lines to Manchester are busy at the moment, I'm afraid, sir.'

'You're not smiling!' he said.

'How can you tell?' she asked in astonishment.
'I can hear it. You're not smiling.'
'Don't be silly. You can't hear a smile.'
'Yes I can. You're smiling now.'
'Trying to connect you.' Her smile was wider as she tried Manchester again. The lines were still busy.
'Lily, please, could we meet?'
'No. We couldn't!' Oh dear, this was getting out of hand.
'Trying to connect you!' she cried desperately.
'Look, Lily, I assure you I'm harmless. I could even get character references if you want. I could ask the bishop, the doctor, the lawyer, the police, the neighbours, the—'
'Stop it, please stop!' she said frantically. At last she made the connection and cut him off.

She was trembling and felt more like crying than smiling. She'd been told about his sort and warned not to get involved. Besides, he had a lady friend he phoned with faithful regularity, long distance in Manchester.

But oh, what a nice voice he had. A voice you could almost fall in love with . . .

Rosie MacDougal's work on the barrows was beset with small irritations since Uncle Sid's stepson Edwin had joined the family. There were arguments daily over Edwin's surname now his ma was married to Sid Hawkins. Edwin said that names were important and contributed to success.

'Just look at Mr Boot, Mr Heinz, Mr Morris and 'Enery Ford – 'ouse'old names that trip off the tongue, Rosie.' He wondered if he should be re-named Hawkins, 'cause that name was more suited to the barrows.

'You can't be a Hawkins!' Rosie objected.

'Why not? I could call meself Rudolph Valentino if I wanted to.'

'I'd die laughing. Anyone less like a film star—!'

'I fancy Edwin Barlow-Hawkins meself,' he mused, ignoring the remark. 'Hyphenated would look swanky on the notepaper when I'm managing director.'

'Oh, come off it, Edwin! How you going to be managing director of anything standing on your hind legs selling onions off a bloomin' barrow?'

He broke off to serve a customer.

'Fresh oranges picked in Jaffa by his 'Ighness the Sheik of Araby hisself, lady. Shilling the 'arf-dozen to you.' She bought a dozen, and went off laughing.

'Yes, Rosie,' he continued, 'Definitely hyphenated. Sir Edwin Hawkins-Barlow sounds posh.'

'Edwin Hawker's-Barrow, more like!' She doubled up laughing and didn't hear another customer approach.

'Glad to see you're happy in your work, Rosie.' Sebastian tapped her on the shoulder.

'Mr Granton!' She went beetroot red. It didn't help that Edwin was watching with keen interest.

'You're very formal all of a sudden!' Sebastian smiled while managing to look hurt.

She was speechless with embarrassment, but Edwin chipped in. 'We're very respectful when speaking to well-dressed young toffs in trilby 'ats, sir. It's a Hawkins rule. What can I do for you?'

'Actually, it's Rosie I came to see.' Sebastian said coldly, sensing a tease. He smiled at her. 'I wondered if you'd like to come dancing with me at the Hammersmith Palais this Saturday, Rosie?'

'Cheaper than taking a working girl to the swanky West End, o' course,' Edwin remarked mildly.

Sebastian flushed with annoyance but pointedly ignored the remark and went on talking to Rosie.

'There's a dancing competition at the Palais this Saturday. I thought it would be a lark to enter. What about it, Rosie?'

'I'd love to, Sebastian!' Her cheeks were rosy as apples and her eyes shone.

'Good-oh!' he said. 'I'll pick you up at seven. Tell your mum you'll be home by twelve, Cinderella!' He laughed and turned away, pausing for a moment to study the barrow. 'I say, those are nice oranges!'

'Only three shillings the 'arf dozen, sir.' Edwin bowed deferentially.

'Edwin . . . !' Rosie hissed furiously.

'To you. Mr Granton,' he said with a smile innocent as a baby's.

Sebastian made sure Gracie knew he was taking Rosie dancing. If Gracie was hurt just because he'd never danced a polka with her, he wanted her to come right out and tell him so. Then they could resume a childhood friendship he'd valued. He imagined he was a pleasant, obliging sort of chap. People liked him, especially girls, so what had he done to offend Gracie MacDougal?

Sebastian was going through a rough patch at the moment and needed to be popular. During the summer holidays he'd worked in his father's office. While studying the books, the size of their bank overdraft had worried him. Sebastian was due to sit accountancy finals next spring, and he knew his father's firm was having problems. It was unsettling, and so was Gracie's indifference.

'Rosie's a jolly good dancer, Gracie. We could win the competition,' Sebastian told her.

'Pass the spanner, will you?' Gracie shrugged.

'MacDougal's Luck' was off the drawing board and in the process of construction. It would be a lighter, speedier vehicle.

'Don't you mind me taking Rosie to the Palais?' Sebastian persisted.

'Why should I? Good luck!'

51

'That nut's too slack,' he grumbled sulkily.

'So you don't trust me to tighten bloomin' hubnuts now, do you?' Gracie gave it another vicious turn. 'Well, I don't care tuppence. I'm only here on sufferance till that man takes my job. Dad gave me the sack, remember?'

'Don't be petulant. Jealousy doesn't suit you.'

She whirled round dangerously with the spanner.

'Jealous? Of you and Rosie? You have too high an opinion of yourself, Mr Granton!'

As soon as the words left her mouth she realized that was word for word what she'd said to young Mr Rampton. But Sebastian would never behave like that horrid young man. They'd been friends for years!

Anger cooled and left her feeling foolish. Pinned to her blouse underneath the overalls was the motor car brooch he'd given her. She wore it often, though Rosie had told her it was only a cheap little brooch similar to one she'd seen in Woolworth's for sixpence. Sebastian cared for her. How could she condemn him because he looked like his father?

'You're impossible!' Sebastian was in a rage. He picked up an oily rag and wiped his hands furiously. 'I can't wait till this mechanic chap arrives and your father sends you off to learn to cook and sew and do whatever it is sensible women do!'

With that, he turned on his heel and left the garage.

'Sebastian gone?' Joseph had heard raised voices and strolled over to investigate.

'He's offended. I told him he'd too high an opinion of himself,' she admitted miserably.

'True!' He laughed. 'Don't look so down in the mouth. Master Granton will bounce back tomorrow, chirpy as you like.'

She didn't think he would. She looked at her dirty hands and grimy fingernails in despair.

'Why does engineering interest me? It's not natural, is it, Dad?'

'Maybe not for a pretty lass, Gracie. But you're descended from a long line of engineers. My own father had a business making farm implements in a blacksmith's near Kelso in the Scottish borders. He trained me and my older brother. A right stern taskmaster he was too!'

'I didn't know you had a brother. You never mentioned him before. You said you'd no relations left in Scotland.' Gracie was curious.

'Yes, well . . .' He looked discomfited.

'Are your family dead?'

'No, Gracie. I checked up when I came home and they're very much alive. It's me that's dead – to them.'

'What do you mean?' She was shocked.

'Forget it! I shouldn't have mentioned them. It was a slip o' the tongue.' Joseph moved restlessly, picking up a spanner she'd left lying on the floor.

'What happened, Dad? Why did—?'

'Leave it, Gracie!' he ordered sternly. 'You don't need to know and it's best forgot anyway.' He gave her a long, hard look. 'I'll thank you not to mention this ever again. Not to me or anyone else – and that includes your mother.'

Gracie had been prepared to hate the new mechanic, but when Evan Jones finally arrived she found that though she might resent his presence, she couldn't hate him. He had a deep Welsh voice, a slow smile and an unruly mop of wavy black hair that was endearing.

The young man limped slightly when following Joseph and Gracie on a tour of the garage. A legacy of his time as a prisoner in the same camp as Joseph MacDougal.

When they came to the partly constructed racing car, Joseph smiled at Gracie, who'd remained silent till now.

'This is our pet project, Evan. Sebastian Granton and

my daughter have been working on it since I designed the new model. Gracie knows more about the engine than I do. She'll explain the finer points.'

'Indeed? That's interesting!' Evan looked Gracie slowly up and down.

Joseph hurried off to attend to a customer and left them together.

'Please don't say women can't be mechanics or I'll scream.' Gracie gave the young man a warning look.

'I wouldn't dream of it, Miss Grace! Didn't we hear nothing in prison camp but Joseph MacDougal singing your praises louder than a Rhondda choir?'

'That means nothing. He's giving you my job because I happen to be a girl. Is that fair?'

'It is not, indeed,' he agreed seriously.

More agreeably, Gracie began to explain the technicalities of 'MacDougal's Luck' Mark 2. Evan asked intelligent questions that showed a wide knowledge of engineering.

Gracie found that reassuring, despite her smouldering resentment. It would be no help to anyone if Evan Jones turned out to be a chump.

Once Joseph's new mechanic had settled in and accepted tenancy of the former groom's cottage, Polly focused attention upon her daughter's future. Her efforts to secure a situation for Gracie with the Grantons met with success, but what would Gracie think about it? Nervously, Polly waited till evening when the family were gathered round the table for supper. If there was to be a blazing row, there was safety in numbers.

'I've spoken to the Grantons' housekeeper, Gracie luv. She says the cook, Bertha Mullins, would gladly take you on. They're short-staffed in the big house. Some housemaids and kitchen maids left to make munitions during the war and never came back.'

Joseph added his support. 'That's a grand chance to

better yourself, Gracie. Bertha Mullins is a famous cook. With your brains, you'll learn fast. Wouldn't be surprised if you open your own fancy restaurant one day.'

Everyone except Gracie laughed.

'Anyway,' said Polly hastily, 'it's up to you, Gracie. Of course if you're dead set against it, we'll have to think again, luv.'

To her relief, Gracie shrugged.

'I don't have much choice, do I?'

Polly allowed silence to speak volumes.

Rosie and Lily were encouraging.

'Neither of us can cook, Gracie,' Rosie said. 'At least, just ordinary cooking like Irish stew and rice pudding. You should give it a try.'

Rosie actually felt quite envious. She hadn't seen Sebastian since they had come badly unstuck during the tango in the dance contest and made idiots of themselves falling over. Gracie would live in comfort in the big house and see him every day, maybe dish up scrambled egg or kippers to him at breakfast. Lucky thing!

'There's only one thing, Gracie . . .' Polly paused for a moment, because this next item had been bothering her. Her Ladyship usually left hiring and firing strictly to the housekeeper, but this time she had asked to see Gracie. It was most unusual!

'Why?' Gracie asked when Polly told her.

Lily giggled. 'To see if your fingernails are clean after pottering around with cars, of course.'

'No, luv.' Polly shot her second daughter a withering look. This was a delicate situation. 'I expect it's just a courtesy because you're my daughter. Lady Frances is a very kind person, you know. Takes a keen interest in all her staff.'

Gracie had never seen such elegant surroundings when her mother ushered her into Lady Frances's suite of rooms next day. Propped up on velvet cushions, the lady lay reading on a low couch. As Polly and Gracie entered she marked the page and put down the book, smiling.

'Come in, Grace. How lovely to see you.' She sounded as if she really meant it.

'Polly, I wonder if you'd mind leaving us alone for fifteen minutes?' Frances Granton glanced at her lady's maid. 'I'd like to get to know your daughter better.'

'Of course, ma'am.' Polly went out and closed the door, confident Gracie would impress the mistress. Her daughter was soberly dressed in a sparkling white blouse and dark-navy skirt, Her coppery hair gleamed and her nails were scrubbed to the quick.

'Twelve inches from the floor.' Lady Frances studied Gracie.

'I beg pardon, ma'am?'

'Your hemline, dear. Very fashionable for 1920. It suits you. Come and sit here beside me, Grace.' She patted a chair close to the couch.

Gracie obeyed. It was strange sitting practically face to face. She felt that Lady Granton could read her every thought.

'Do you really want to be a kitchen maid?' Frances Granton asked directly.

'What else can I do? My father won't have me in the garage because I'm a woman and the bicycle factory gave me the sack.'

'Why was that?'

Gracie hesitated. She'd told no one about young Mr Rampton's awful behaviour, but those blue eyes were compelling!

'My boss took too keen an interest in the assembly line girls. I hit him with a brolly.'

'Ah, I see!' Lady Frances's lips twitched. 'But last time we spoke you had ambitions. What happened to those?'

'They were daydreams, ma'am. I just want to be an ordinary sensible person now,' she said quietly, remembering an angry, contemptuous Sebastian.

'Oh, nonsense, Grace!' Frances Granton scoffed. 'You could never be ordinary. Mind you, I do admire sensible women. I was never one. I was a spoiled little madam who couldn't boil an egg and thought nothing of dancing the night away. And sometimes I'm jolly glad I did when I had the chance!' She sighed. 'Anyway, I suppose what I'm trying to say is, if you have the brains to be a first-class engineer, forget about learning to boil eggs and go and do it, for heaven's sake!'

Gracie thought about her mother and Sir William and the weight of responsibility she owed this poor wronged lady.

'I *have* to work here, ma'am. I have to . . . er . . . look after my mother.'

Oh dear, had she said too much?

They stared at one another. Gracie couldn't tell what the lady was thinking.

'Don't worry, Grace, I'll take care of your mother myself,' Lady Granton said at last.

'Tell me honestly—' She leaned forward, looking directly at the silent girl. 'If you didn't have to work in my kitchen, if you were a free agent, what would you do?'

Gracie didn't have to give that a second thought. The words came out, unbidden.

'I'd go to Scotland. My father has relatives there who have an engineering business. I'd ask them to give me a job, ma'am. I don't know if they would, but I'd like to try. Dad's told me a little about them and – and about how beautiful Scotland is.' She said nothing about a family feud. She'd promised her father not to, and anyway what was the point? The whole plan was impossible.

'If that's what you want, Grace, I'll help you.' Lady Frances looked at her thoughtfully.

'Oh, no, ma'am!' She was taken aback. 'It's kind, but I couldn't ask you to do that!'

'Oh yes, you could,' Lady Frances said decisively.

And Gracie knew that somehow she'd arrange it. Maybe quite soon she could be meeting her father's folk. The very thought made Gracie's heart beat faster.

Four

Polly came bustling into the room when the fifteen minutes were up. She could tell right away the interview had gone well. Lady Granton and Grace were sitting together, chummy as you like.

'Well, ma'am, have you told our Gracie what's expected of her?' she smiled.

'Gracie knows what I want her to do.' Frances Granton gave Gracie a significant look. 'Don't you, dear?'

'Yes, ma'am,' she answered dutifully. The visit to Scotland would remain their secret.

'Don't worry, Polly,' Lady Granton smiled. 'I'll make sure Gracie has a variety of work experience.'

Polly was bursting with pride. 'She'll learn quicker than ordinary, ma'am. Our Gracie has brains.'

'How unusual!' the lady remarked mildly. There was an amused twinkle in her eye that made Gracie hide a smile.

Fortunately Polly missed the joke. She was busy giving her daughter a meaningful glance designed to get her on her feet and out of there.

'Will you be wanting afternoon tea now, ma'am?' she asked.

'That'd be nice, my dear. With perhaps a finger of Cook's shortbread to remind me of Scotland,' Frances Granton said innocently.

Gracie started work at Granton House a few days later. It was decided she would live in servants' quarters, more convenient for a 5.30 a.m. start. She was given an attic room and two sets of uniform, one for morning, the other fancier for afternoon and evening. She was also fitted with two pairs of rubber-soled shoes. 'So's you don't clump around disturbing the gentry,' Cook explained.

Her duties were simple enough. In the morning she cleaned out ashes and filled coal scuttles before helping to serve breakfast. Later on, once she'd mastered breakfasts, she might progress to luncheons and dinners. It felt strange, giving Sebastian breakfast. She was told to sound the gong promptly at 7.30 a.m. and pounded it with such tremendous gusto the first morning, he came down with sticking plaster on his chin, having cut himself shaving.

He scowled when he saw her standing by the sideboard.

'Good morning, Grace,' Sir William said smiling kindly at the new maid. 'I hope you'll be happy with us. We're very pleased to have you and your mother working here. Makes it quite a family affair, doesn't it?'

'Yes, sir.' She wondered if he saw the irony.

'What's for breakfast?' Sebastian asked.

'Bacon and egg.'

'Nothing else?'

'Kippers – sir,' Gracie said. Their eyes met. This was ridiculous! It was a struggle not to laugh as she served his choice of two fried eggs and bacon. She hoped he approved of her sensible demeanour.

Sebastian did not. This was the most awkward breakfast he'd ever eaten. He kept catching her eye, sparkling with mischief although her expression was impassive. His appetite was ruined.

Frances Granton was not one to rush things. Always a clever strategist, she allowed time to pass before making a move she'd been considering for some time.

Her husband visited her room every evening after work

and sat with her for an hour or so before dinner. William found Frances's quiet presence relaxing. If she happened to ask, he made light of business worries, though of late she had noted observantly how tired and careworn he seemed. Enough was enough, Frances decided one evening.

'Have you managed to reduce the overdraft?' she demanded.

'My dear! Who told you about that?' William was surprised. He'd kept that particular worry to himself.

'Sebastian is more forthcoming than you are, William.'

'He shouldn't have troubled you!'

'Oh yes, he should. I may be weak in body, but there's nothing wrong with my brain.' She glanced at him. 'Why not sell the Scottish estate? Wouldn't that help?'

'Oh yes!' He studied her doubtfully. 'But I thought you'd never consider selling our Scottish home, my darling! It's where we spent our honeymoon, remember?'

'The honeymoon ended long ago,' she said quietly. 'We've been absentee landlords too long. Time to give the land back to those who love it.'

'Maybe you're right.' William couldn't meet her eyes.

'I know I am. The house will need a thorough clean though, if it's to appeal to a prospective buyer.'

'The caretaker and his wife are too old to tackle that job!'

'I thought we could send Biddy Hagerty and young Gracie MacDougal to give them a hand. Biddy has raised cleaning to a fine art, and Gracie is hard working and sensible. I'm very pleased with the girl. It will be good experience for her.'

'D'you know, Frances, I believe you've saved our bacon.' He leaned across gratefully and kissed his wife. Could it be that their money worries were over?

She settled back on the couch contentedly after he'd gone. That was one problem solved, at least . . .

When Sebastian was told of his father's plans to sell the Scottish estate it lifted a load off his shoulders, knowing the family's financial difficulties – yet the loss saddened him. He'd loved holidays there, but it was true that since his mother's illness they'd visited Scotland less and less.

He was surprised to learn Gracie MacDougal was to travel to Scotland to help spring-clean the house. When questioned, his mother was vague and couldn't say how long Biddy and Gracie would be gone. It unsettled Sebastian. He had grown accustomed to Gracie working around the place and teasing him with a straight face. He quite enjoyed it now. Seeing her in maid's uniform bothered him though, it didn't seem right somehow. He didn't know why.

Gracie sang softly off-key while she worked. She always had. Gracie's tone-deaf singing had been part of Sebastian's childhood and growing up. Since she came, every morning while shaving he would detect the faint murmur of her flat little song as she prepared breakfast, and it made him smile. Silly, but he'd miss the absorbed little sound once she'd gone.

He located Gracie in the library one morning prior to her departure. She had dusters and furniture polish nearby, but was leaning on her elbows studying an atlas open on the table.

'So you're off to Scotland!' he challenged her and she jumped.

'I wish you wouldn't sneak up on me like that, Sebastian. It's us servants who're meant to sneak around, not you posh people.'

'Why are they sending you to Scotland with old ma Hagerty?' he grumbled. 'You've only been here a few weeks. Aren't you on probation still?'

'No.' She closed the atlas. 'I've been passed as hard-working and sensible. That's what you wanted, wasn't it?'

62

He wrinkled his nose. 'It's awfully dull.'

'Make up your mind!' She replaced the atlas and polished the table.

'Everything shines since you came, Gracie, and you do lovely breakfasts,' he said, hoping to please.

Her eyes gleamed balefully. 'Glad to give satisfaction – *sir*!'

'I'll miss you while you're gone, you know.'

'Hard luck! Why not ask Rosie to the Palais to take your mind off elbow grease and ham and eggs?'

He drew himself up, hurt and angry. 'Maybe I will!' He ran a hand along a high bookshelf and held up blackened fingertips. 'Dust!' he said accusingly and stormed out.

Gracie grabbed a duster and furiously attacked the shelf. A few humiliated tears escaped, mingled with the dust of ages.

Joseph MacDougal was worried. He asked his mechanic to keep an eye on the garage for ten minutes. 'Just want a word with the missus about the sale of the Grantons' Scottish estate, Evan. What a bombshell!'

'Indeed it is,' the young man agreed. 'The kitchen was in a tizzy when I was in, fearing the collapse of Granton's altogether.'

'Oh, it won't come to that. I suppose it makes sense to sell the estate, now Lady Frances is too poorly to travel.'

Evan Jones was sorry for his old friend. He suspected Joseph's real concern was Gracie. She was being packed off to Scotland, and there was much speculation in the kitchen as to why. Apparently Gracie and Sebastian Granton had been overheard having words in the library, after which Gracie appeared tearful and upset. Kitchen staff thrive on scandal, but Evan did not believe the colourful rumours going around. He had formed his own high opinion of Grace MacDougal's resolute morals.

Polly had arrived home to prepare the evening meal when Joseph burst in. She was surprised. 'You're early!'

'Just a quick word before the girls get back. It's about Gracie being sent to Scotland. What's behind it, Polly?'

'Nothing. She's a hard-working girl. The housekeeper told me Lady Frances wants someone sensible to go with Biddy Hagerty to clean the old house. Gracie was the obvious choice. Those other giddy goats in the kitchen would be off to the dancing most nights.'

'Yes, I know, but there's a rumour she's being sent away in disgrace because of a carry-on with Sebastian Granton.'

'Rubbish!' Polly was emphatic. 'Gracie has no time for him. Sebastian asks Rosie out occasionally, of course, but only because she's a good dancer.'

'There's temptation when a couple are under the same roof, though!' he persisted.

The colour left Polly's face. Does he suspect? she wondered in guilty terror. But he was smiling as he went on.

'Still, I know for a fact, our Gracie wouldn't put up with any nonsense from Master Sebastian! Did you know she hit young Mr Rampton with a brolly when he tried to get fresh?'

'No!'

'It's true. That's why she got the sack. The foreman told me the story's all round the factory, and the man Rampton's a laughing stock.'

'Serves him right!' Polly smiled. 'We needn't worry unduly about Gracie going to Scotland then.'

'No. Seems she can look after herself,' Joseph said uneasily, not at all reassured.

'Meeting will come to order,' said Grandpa Hawkins sternly, rapping on the board and frowning at Rosie, who was laughing.

64

The Hawkinses were attending a board meeting. It was raining cats and dogs outside, pattering overhead on the glass roof of the shopping arcade. Grandma and Grandpa Hawkins were present, so were Uncle Sid, Edwin and Rosie. The board was laid across trestles on the Hawkins' arcade pitch and Edwin was holding forth about a book he'd been reading on salesmanship, aimed at attracting customers.

'Lighting's important,' he went on after the interruption. ''Orrible October day like this, you want customers to view Sid's fruit, Grandpa's veg and Grandma's flowers as if they was in sunshine. Cheers customers up no end, good lighting does. Puts 'em in buying mood.'

Rosie yawned. 'If they have any money to buy with, poor souls. Nobody has these days. Land fit for heroes? I'll eat my 'at!'

'Defeatist talk.' Edwin shook his head sadly. 'Never get bread buttered with that attitude, my girl.'

'Boy's right,' Grandma nodded. 'Mind you, Grandpa and me never had no fancy lighting but we always kept sunny smiles on. Even when our feet was killing us, we did. Same idea.'

'But much less expensive,' Rosie said.

'Got to move with the times, Rosie girl.' Grandpa Hawkins was undisputed chairman of the board. 'Take a leaf out of Mr Woolworth's book and plough profits back into business. Couple of electric light bulbs wouldn't break the bank.'

'What about the barrows outside?' she argued. 'You can't light barrows with electric.'

'That's where your cheap sunny smile comes in, duckie.' Edwin grinned. 'I suggest Grandpa and Sid man the arcade pitch, this being the Hawkins' flagship, so to speak. Grandma could have the small barrow to show pretty posies and bouquets in the warm just inside the entrance, while you and me, Rosie, braves the helements streetside, with fruit and veg.'

'Us, alone?'

'I could ask me ma to chaperone, and I don't think,' he mocked. 'Oh, and we should all wear similar gear. I propose white shirts, green an' white striped aprons and straw boaters trimmed with red ribbon. Very keen on workers wearing similar gear, was dear old Mr Heinz.'

'Oh blimey, boaters!' groaned Rosie. What would Sebastian think?

'All those in favour, 'ands up!' Grandpa Hawkins cried. 'Motion carried with one abstention!' he declared, glaring at Rosie.

To signify close of meeting, he ceremonially draped the bare board with grass-green cloth. That had been one of Edwin's earlier suggestions, and certainly showed fruit and veg to best advantage.

Working on the main switchboard, Lily MacDougal was apprehensive in case her admirer called again. Fortunately another operator handled his next call and Lily was spared embarrassment. After that there was a long silence. None of her friends on the switchboard reported dealing with that particular Manchester number. She wondered if her curt refusal to meet had persuaded her caller to conduct his love affair with the Manchester lady by letter, instead of entrusting tender thoughts to the telephone while flirting with the operator.

All the same his silence bothered her. He hadn't sounded the sort they warned operators against. Trustworthy was a word that sprang to mind in describing the tone of voice.

Which is nonsense, Lily thought. How can you trust a voice? But he could tell I was smiling, so isn't it just possible I could tell he was trustworthy? she reasoned. How confusing it was!

She didn't smile quite so readily these days. His voice lingered at the back of her mind, like a teasing whisper.

When he turned up again she was caught by surprise.

'Directory Enquiries, please, miss!'

'Why, it's you!' Lily cried, laughing. Laughter was a serious lapse of professional conduct, but it was a dreary autumn day and his voice seemed like a ray of sunshine on a dull afternoon.

'Lily! Look, I'm terribly sorry I embarrassed you last time. Trouble is, I'm afraid I can't forget you.'

'Don't be silly!' She wondered if he could hear her smile. 'How can you remember me if we've never met?'

'That's not my fault, is it?'

She paused. If the supervisor heard her she'd get the sack for sure, but there was something she had to know.

'What about the lady in Manchester?'

'She's in London now. Handy for me. I need a phone number to rent a flat.'

'Oh, I see,' she said cuttingly. 'I'll put you through at once to Directory Enquiries, sir.'

'Lily, wait! Why are you angry?'

'Why should you care? I'm just a voice!'

'A voice I can't forget.'

'Why are voices important to you anyway?' she demanded crossly. 'Are you an actor or a singer or something?'

'Bit of all three.' She could hear him smile. 'Listen, Lily, I believe we should meet,' he went on. 'Curiosity demands it, if nothing else. Do you have any free time?'

She hesitated. She should refuse, but she had to admit she was curious. 'I have a Wednesday afternoon off on 27th October. We mustn't meet at the Telephone Exchange though. That's frowned on.'

'Very well. You know the church just round the corner, the one with twin spires? There's a small arched gateway by the main entrance. I'll wait there at two o'clock on the 27th. I'll wait for an hour in case you're delayed.'

'All right,' she agreed breathlessly. She caught sight of the supervisor approaching and hurriedly made the connection. It was only after she'd done it and he'd gone she realized she'd forgotten to ask his name.

Sebastian offered to drive Gracie and Biddy Hagerty to the station, but Joseph MacDougal turned down the offer. Evan Jones drove them instead.

'Your father is worried about you,' Evan remarked to Gracie, who was sitting beside him. Biddy had an assortment of cleaning materials and utensils with her and there was no room in the back.

'I can look after myself,' Gracie said.

'So I heard.' He cast a swift glance at the brolly clutched in one hand. He changed thoughtfully to a lower gear in the heavy London traffic. 'But I'm thinking that's not Joseph's fear, Grace, it's whether you'll find a welcome in Scotland. If you don't, you'll be upset – and if you do, you'll not come home.'

'I'll always come home, Evan.'

He pulled up outside the station and turned to look at her. 'But that depends where home is, does it not?'

It was a long train journey, complicated by changes from the express to a chugging local train, lumbered as they were with Biddy's packages and bundles. But once they reached the borders, the high Scottish hills were waiting, clothed in misty evening beauty that took Gracie's breath away. Walter Marcus, the old caretaker, met their train at Netholm with a pony and trap. If he was dismayed by Mrs Hagerty's Vim, soda crystals and Jeyes Fluid, he gave no sign.

'Me and Matty are pleased they're selling the old place,' he confided, shaking up the reins to make the old pony trot. 'Shame to see the house standing empty and the land not properly tended. Should be a lot of interest. Besides good grazing, there's fishing rights on the river that should fetch a pretty penny.'

'Won't you miss it, Mr Marcus?' Gracie asked.

'Nah. Sir William wrote there's a cottage in Coldstream earmarked for us near our daughter in recognition o' long service.'

'That's more thoughtful than most,' Biddy Hagerty remarked.

'Decent people the Grantons. Honourable man, Sir William,' the old man nodded.

Gracie said nothing, staring straight ahead.

Work began in earnest next morning. It was a big house, but not too big to be a comfortable home. Gracie admired it, though everything was shabby and dusty. You could imagine children enjoying the freedom of the spacious rooms and romping in the garden, mostly laid out in grass short-cropped by sheep. She tried to imagine Sebastian playing here as a child, but all she saw was a small boy wandering in loneliness. She gave herself an impatient shake to dispel the image.

'Right, Biddy. Where do we start?'

'Where else but the attics, dearie?'

They toiled to the top of the house with mops, brushes and bundles of sacks for rubbish. Matty Marcus followed, unlocking doors as she went. 'Not much stored up here with it being a holiday home,' she said, looking round dusty, cobwebby attics. 'Mostly broken old pieces of furniture fit for a bonfire. We'll put them in the lobby and Wally and the shepherd can carry them down.'

Soon the skylights were open and fresh air was blowing through. When the rubbish had been cleared and the floors washed, all that was left were a few pieces of furniture Biddy and Matty considered good enough to keep, Sebastian's toys for him to sort out and a leather photograph album. 'Best take the album downstairs for the family to see to, Gracie,' Matty said. 'Photos are personal. They wouldn't want them included in the roup.'

She went on to explain to the Londoners a roup was a Scottish auction, and house contents and estate machinery would go under the hammer when the place was sold. It was sad, Gracie thought as she carried the dusty book downstairs.

All through the next busy week they worked cleaning bedrooms, bathrooms, cupboards and public rooms. Matty enlisted the help of a washerwoman and every day the women washed, ironed, scrubbed, dusted and polished till the old house fairly gleamed from attic to cellar. Sunday was a day of rest and a blessed relief, Gracie thought. Every muscle ached and her hands were red and roughened with washing soda. They attended church in Coldstream with Walter and Matty, then Biddy announced she intended getting her head down for the afternoon. Gracie was left to her own devices.

She wandered through the house, admiring the quiet rooms till she came to one lined with bookshelves which served as library and games room. The photograph album lay on a shelf and she lifted it down and settled in a chair to study the pages.

First of all were Frances and William Granton's wedding photographs – bride, groom and attendants posed woodenly. Yet somehow the joy and happiness of the young couple shone through the formality. Frances and William were obviously very much in love. She was lovely, he was handsome, their hands so tightly clasped it seemed nothing could ever part them.

Yet cruel illness had driven them apart – and so had Polly MacDougal. Gracie turned the page, her heart sore. The next photographs were taken in the grounds of the estate, probably on honeymoon. These were less formal and positively glowed with happiness. Frances danced on the lawn in William's arms, a spaniel pup frolicking round them. Another showed them dressed in waders and oilskins, knee-deep in the river, clinging together while he taught her to fish. There were picnics in the sun with young friends, several scenes riding bicycles in quiet country lanes, and a wonderful shot of the honeymooners on horseback high in the hills, outlined against the evening sky.

Gracie closed the book gently, tears on her lashes. If only her mother could see this!

By the end of the week Biddy was satisfied there was nothing left to clean, inside or out.

'What now, Biddy?' Gracie asked.

'Well—' she frowned – 'her ladyship told me – though it would be a great loss to Granton House, you understand – she believed my place was back home in Ireland. And didn't she hint she would applaud if I handed in my notice and sailed from Scotland after this job was done? There's nothing to hold me in London, now my dear Liam's gone, and I do worry about my old mother in Donegal with unrest and riots in the country.'

'Did she mention me, Biddy?' Gracie asked.

'She did indeed. She hoped you'd grab the chance to visit your father's relatives.' She rummaged in a capacious handbag and brought out a fat envelope. 'By the by, Gracie, here's your pay packet. I have mine and it's more than generous, bless 'er kind heart. Enough to see me across the sea and buy comforts for my mother.'

'You're leaving then?'

'Oh yes, my dear,' Biddy said happily. 'I'm leaving.'

After helping Biddy compose a heartfelt letter to Lady Frances, Gracie was still undecided what she should do. She had a return ticket to London in her purse, but she had family quite close and longed to meet them. Thoughts of a feud were daunting though, and her father had warned her

71

not to meddle. Should she disobey him, or return meekly home and face Lady Frances's displeasure?

First, however, she had a tearful Biddy to see off to catch the train to Stranraer. Gracie stood outside the house watching Biddy Hagerty's white hanky flutter goodbye as Walter drove her away in the pony trap. With Biddy gone, she felt lost.

Frances Granton had urged her to fight for what she wanted, but the dear lady had not known the hostility she could face. If only I knew what Dad had done, she thought. Was it so terrible?

Gracie wandered back into the house. Walter and Matty lived in a nearby cottage, so she had the big house to herself. She made a pot of tea and drank a cup seated in the shining kitchen. The house cat jumped on to her lap and settled, purring. There was nothing to be heard but the tick of the clock and she must have dozed, because a loud knocking wakened her. The cat shot off her knee and disappeared upstairs. Stifling a yawn, she opened the back door.

'Evan Jones!' she gasped.

Gracie could hardly believe he was here, smiling at her, but as if to prove it wasn't a dream, the open-topped Sunbeam her father had recently purchased stood in the yard.

'Blimey, Evan, you've had a long drive!' she laughed delightedly.

'Long enough,' he smiled.

'No breakdowns, no punctures?' She ushered him in and took his coat.

'Not one. Roads are improving and so are tyres – thanks to Mr Dunlop.' He accepted a cup of tea gratefully.

'Now, Evan,' she said, settling down opposite. 'What on earth are you doing in Scotland?'

'It's the miners' strike, Grace. Train services could be

disrupted, so your father sent me to bring you and Mrs Hagerty home.'

'She's gone back to Donegal.'

'Then isn't it a blessing I came?'

A blessing? she wondered. Had Dad an ulterior motive in mind?

'I want to visit my Scottish relations first though, Evan.' she said.

'Ah! Your father said you might. He didn't advise it, you know.'

'I suppose he told you about the family row?'

'Yes. He seemed to think you'd be upset if you went.'

'It's not fair, involving you,' she said. 'You'll get the blame whatever I do.'

'I have a broad back.' He shrugged.

'Well, anyway,' she sighed. 'You must stay here tonight. There's plenty room.'

'It is indeed a beautiful house.'

'You should have seen it before Mrs Hagerty came here!'

'And you, Grace,' he added smiling. 'Your presence would grace any house.'

She gave him a startled glance, but his expression was guarded and she couldn't tell what he was thinking.

'Tomorrow morning I'll check the engine before we make the return journey.'

'Can I help?' she offered.

'Oh yes indeed. I was counting on it.' He grinned.

They rose early next day. It was strange making breakfast for Evan. It reminded her that she was just a servant. Would she want to return to that job for the rest of her days?

They garaged the Austin under cover in the empty stables because there was room to work and ominous rainclouds had gathered overnight. Gracie was happily absorbed checking the immaculate engine. She sang as she worked.

'You would not be invited to join the Rhondda choir, my girl,' Evan chuckled. 'But I like the sound, like contented purring.'

'Sebastian says my singing lies somewhere between a London taxicab and a Model T Ford.' She laughed.

'You're fond of him, aren't you?' he said, watching her.

'We quarrel, mostly.' She frowned. 'He fancies Rosie because she can dance. He's a good dancer, you know.'

'You think dancing is important? I have two left feet and a broken leg badly set in prison camp, but I'll learn if you want me to.'

'Don't be daft!' she said awkwardly. She stood up, wiping her hands.

'The engine's fine, Evan. I'll put the kettle on.'

She escaped into the yard and walked briskly towards the house. At the doorway she stood for a moment breathing the scented country air. The scene before her was peaceful, hills with a backdrop of dramatic dark clouds. She'd miss all this, in London!

'Oh, there you are, Gracie,' Sebastian Granton said casually, emerging through the doorway. 'I wondered where everyone was.'

'Where did *you* come from?' Her heart lurched with shock.

'Aren't you delighted?'

'No. You gave me a fright.'

'Mother suggested I come and rescue you. The miners are on strike and railworkers threatening to join in. They want a two shilling rise and I hope they get it. I drove north in a Morris Father just bought. Cracking little car, Gracie. You'll love it.'

'If I ever sit in it.'

'Course you will,' he said confidently. 'Mother said to drive you around as much as you want while I'm here, visit your father's birthplace, meet your relatives and all that. You've earned a holiday, Gracie, the house looks absolutely splendid.'

'You could thank Mrs Hagerty, but she's gone back home to Ireland.'

'So we're alone!'

'We-ell . . .'

Evan chose that moment to come into the yard. He'd heard voices and was curious. The two young men stared at one another and Sebastian's expression darkened. He rounded on Gracie accusingly.

'What's going on? My mother trusted you, Grace!'

'I can see you don't!' she retorted indignantly.

'The evidence is before my eyes.' He scowled at Evan. 'You've been here all alone with him!'

'Oh, I see! And it's all right to be all alone with you, is it?' she said cuttingly.

'Yes, of course. This is my house.'

'I do not like your tone, Mr Granton.' Evan was looking dangerous. 'For myself, I would ignore your remarks as beneath contempt, but I will not let you insult this young lady. You will apologize.'

'Lady?' Sebastian yelled indignantly. 'Good heavens, man, don't be putting Gracie on a pedestal. She won't like it. She's my friend, not a simpering debutante in high heels! And if you want an apology from me because you're ogling Gracie, you won't get it!'

'Why, you—!'

'Stop it!' Gracie panted, struggling to keep the two apart. 'Evan arrived yesterday afternoon to drive me home, Sebastian. My father had the same thought as your mother, so he sent Evan. And we're leaving right now.'

'Leaving?' Sebastian repeated stupidly.

'Yes. Soon as I've collected my things!' she told him angrily.

Gracie was good as her word, packing hastily and climbing into the Sunbeam beside Evan, while Sebastian stood glowering. Watching him, her mood softened. After all, he had called her his friend. She didn't know he cared!

'It was kind of you to come all the way from London, Sebastian. Thank you.'

'Don't thank me.' His eyes were cold. 'I wanted to check the house anyway to make sure nothing was stolen.'

'Oohh!' she gasped.

The implication behind the words was a calculated insult and she doubted if she would ever forgive it. Evan drove off with an angry squeal of tyres while Gracie sat straight-backed. She did not look back.

When they had reached the Coldstream road, Evan slowed the car and glanced at Gracie. He could not bear to see her in tears.

'Look,' he said gently, 'Kelso is not far. If you want to visit your relatives I'll take you. It seems a pity not to make the effort just because of a quarrel that had nothing to do with you.'

She met his concerned gaze. He was a friend indeed when a friendship had just ended in humiliation.

'Thank you, Evan. I'd like that,' she said gratefully.

He turned the wheel, and soon they were heading across country. Patchy sunlight escaped through gaps in rain-laden clouds, enough to brighten and cheer the landscape with glowing autumnal colour. She began to take an interest in countryside which must have been familiar to her father. She considered it wild, hilly and beautiful, with here and there glimpses of the river Tweed, fast-flowing after rain in the hills. Why had her father never returned, or brought his wife and family to visit his beautiful birthplace?

The family feud of course! That stupid feud . . .

'Look, There it is!' Evan cried suddenly, slowing down.

Gracie craned her head eagerly. They were approaching a town which must be Kelso, dominated by a large castle which must be the one she'd noticed on the atlas. Floors, it was called. But it wasn't that fine edifice that made her catch her breath.

'Oh, Evan!' she gasped.

Once perhaps, the MacDougals had started with just a modest roadside smiddy. Gracie could even make out the original doorway, wide enough for Clydesdale horses to pass through, but the original small stone building now served as smart offices adjoining a much larger and more substantial engineering works. She saw the bright blueish flame of acetylene welding going on inside and heard the high whine of machinery. Across the front of the building in large metal letters was the legend 'MACDOUGAL'.

Evan had drawn into the side and stopped the car. 'This is where Joseph should be!' he said quietly, surveying the prosperous business.

Where *I* should be! Gracie added silently.

She scanned the complex eagerly, but to her disappointment there was nobody about, nor anyone to be seen in the glass-fronted showroom displaying complicated farm machinery.

Behind the works, however, she glimpsed a garden and a house set back from the road. By this time her stomach was churning with excitement and nerves.

'Should I make myself known?' She looked at Evan uncertainly.

'You'll regret it if you don't.' He laid a hand on hers. 'Go on, Grace. They will meet you and be captivated, and if they are not, they are not worth knowing!'

'Will you wait for me?' She smiled shakily.

'For as long as it takes,' he promised.

It was a square stone house, sturdy rather than beautiful,

Gracie thought. She approached warily, her feet crunching noisily through gravel on the path. Somewhere a dog barked. Were they watching her and wondering who she could be? Her hand trembled as she pressed the doorbell.

They must have been watching, because the door was opened within seconds and a man stood looking out. The resemblance to her father was so marked it made Gracie take a step back. But she judged this man to be older.

'Good afternoon, miss.' He smiled pleasantly. 'What can I do for you?' He glanced towards the Sunbeam, visible through trees. 'Has your car broken down?'

Gracie took a deep breath. 'No, sir, the car's fine. I'm Joseph MacDougal's daughter. I – I believe, perhaps, you are my uncle?'

His expression changed and he glared for a long, startled moment before taking a quick, menacing step forward.

'You mean Joseph sent you? He has the cheek of the devil, sending a lass to speak for him!'

'No!' she cried in distress. 'No, he didn't. Please listen—'

'No, my lass, you listen!' He thrust his head forward angrily. 'Take a message to your father. You may tell my brother neither he nor his kin are welcome in this house!'

Five

'Oh, please!' Gracie cried as she watched the door close. She visualized a working life spent cleaning other people's houses, cooking other people's meals. She knew something essential to her being would shrivel and die.

Her uncle hesitated, and they stood looking at one another.

'I don't even know what my father's supposed to have done,' she said.

'Supposed? Oh, my dear lassie!' He gave a bitter little bark of laughter, but he spoke kindly. Under different circumstances, she believed they could have worked together, even have grown to like one another. 'Look, it's not your fault,' he went on reasonably. 'It's just the sight of you brings back memories this family doesn't want resurrected. We grieved for your father when he went as if he'd died too. It's best left that way for the old lady's sake.'

'What old lady?'

'I suppose – your grandmother,' he said reluctantly. He straightened his shoulders, became businesslike. 'Now you'd better be on your way, Miss MacDougal. Your car's waiting and there's nothing here for you. I'm sorry.'

As the door closed she heard a woman's voice within call a question. 'Only a lassie asking directions, Mother,' she heard him answer. That seemed to set the final seal on the encounter.

Gracie walked slowly back to the Sunbeam. There were even more unanswered questions now. Her uncle hadn't said much, but what he had let slip bothered her. He'd said they'd mourned for her father *too*, but who else had died, and why was Joseph MacDougal an outcast? All sorts of awful possibilities flashed through her mind.

Evan Jones didn't have to ask how the meeting went, the failure was evident as she climbed back in the car.

'I told you they weren't worth knowing.' He reached for her hand.

'I spoke to my uncle, Evan,' she said in a choked little voice. 'He wanted nothing to do with me. If he'd only given me a chance. I'm sure we could have got along.'

'It's the man's loss not yours.' Evan shrugged. 'Did he say what the family quarrel was about?'

'No, I'm none the wiser. Except that it's something tragic they don't want to remember.' Gracie looked confused. I suppose if I stayed I'd be a constant reminder. You can see their point.'

'Looking at your sweet face, I cannot!'

It was consolation to know Evan admired her, but it was a complication Gracie could do without at the moment.

'Anyway,' she said hastily, 'I discovered I have another Grandma. Dad led us to believe she was dead.'

'His own mother?' He was incredulous. 'How could he?'

'Look, Evan!' Gracie had caught sight of something going on. 'Someone's just left the house.'

They watched a young man walk briskly up the path to the road, then make a detour hidden by trees and bushes till he crossed the road farther down. He reached Gracie's side of the car by means of this devious route. She rolled down the window and he put one foot on the running board and an elbow on the window ledge. He was dark-haired and smiling, but the dark brown eyes nearly level with her own were not MacDougal eyes, which were shades of blue.

'You're Joseph MacDougal's daughter, I heard you tell Angus,' he said.

'Then you'll have heard the welcome I got. Are you a MacDougal?'

'No, I'm James Cameron. I'm employed here in the works.'

'You mean you're an engineer?'

'More of a designer.' He smiled. 'I helped build tanks during the war, which led to designing farm tractors in peacetime.'

'So all three of us are engineers of one kind or another,' Evan said.

'You mean Miss MacDougal as well?' It was the stranger's turn to look intrigued.

'Oh yes. Gracie's a very talented engineer. She's worked in her father's garage since she was tiny.'

'Your father's garage?' James Cameron studied Gracie. 'An interest in engineering's unusual for a young lady.'

'I suppose engineering's in the blood,' she sighed. 'Along with a long memory for grudges. I'd hoped to persuade my uncle to give me a job but my feet barely touched the ground.'

'Ah yes. The feud!' His brown eyes took on a guarded look as if weighing the risk of involvement in dangerous matters. He seemed to make up his mind suddenly. 'There's somebody I think you ought to meet.'

'Who is it?' Gracie sat up.

'My mother actually.' He glanced at Evan with a winning smile. 'Would you be a sport and give us a lift to Kelso?'

It wasn't far. Evan drove down over cobbles into a town bordering the river, past castle gates that were a masterpiece of ironwork. Gracie looked around with interest at buildings which must have been familiar to her father. A school, a ruined abbey and a church, well-built stone terraces and houses, shops around a pleasant town centre, a stretch of the broad river Tweed nearby.

James Cameron, seated in the back, leaned forward between them giving directions. 'Stop here,' he ordered, indicating a square stone house on two storeys, standing in its own garden in a quiet back street.

Gracie clambered out and stood uncertainly on the pavement. The men joined her. 'Come on in, Miss MacDougal.' James Cameron took her arm, but Evan checked him with a hand on the chest.

'This visit may not concern me, Mr Cameron, but I will not leave Gracie alone with you.'

'You think I'm not to be trusted?' He grinned.

'I am not a man to be taking chances.'

'Then you're welcome to come.' James Cameron laughed. 'Follow me.' He did not approach the front door but led them round to the back, which consisted of a big neatly kept garden – in reality a large drying green. It was surrounded by bushy herbs in faded autumn colours. Gracie recognized light green fever few, darker basil, purple sage and a great faded hedge of lavender. Closer to the house lay a compact vegetable garden well endowed with healthy cabbages, cauliflower and sprouts. The drying green contained a regiment of clothes poles and more white sheets than Gracie had seen for many a day, all flapping in the breeze on an intricate criss-cross of washing lines.

'My mother takes in washing, and sometimes lodgers – if they pass strict vetting procedures.' James smiled, following the direction of her eyes. 'Come and meet her. She'll be ironing, but at this time of day she'll have the kettle on.'

He opened the back door and led them into a lime-coated wash-house containing two wash boilers, four huge sinks and a large upright mangle beside two empty wickerwork baskets of equally gargantuan proportions. Two pulleys occupied the entire ceiling and obviously took care of bad weather. The room was heated by the idling boilers, and big sash windows either side gave airy ventilation. Leather satchels of clothes pegs hung neatly on nearby hooks. The whole area had a businesslike feel which Gracie appreciated. She breathed in a clean smell of soap and washing soda mingled with lavender as they passed through, their footsteps ringing on a red-tiled floor.

Their host opened a door leading off the wash-house and they found themselves in a big kitchen-cum-living room stretching from front to back of the house. At first glance, it looked to Gracie like a hive of industry – then she realized the illusion was created by quite a small person moving fast.

'It's me, Ma.'

'Oh, hello, James dear. Didn't expect you so soon.'

'These two gave me a lift from the works.'

'Kind of them.' She glanced up and smiled but the iron didn't stop till she'd finished a pillowcase spread out upon the widest, strangest ironing board Gracie had ever seen. It had all sorts of attachments, whose use she could only guess at.

The woman's quick glance took in Gracie's interest and the smile widened.

'James invented it for me. Clever isn't it? You can iron sleeves, shirt collars, frills, pleats or sheets, no bother at all.'

She replaced the flat iron in a row of others varying in size from large to tiny which sat at the back of the range, then put the pillowcase on a similar pile. The room was fragrant with the smell of freshly laundered linen and the all-pervading scent of lavender.

'Well, that's it till the next lot dries, rain permitting. Now, James, introduce us.' She spoke the way she worked, quickly and economically. He turned to Gracie first, and she sensed suppressed excitement.

'Mother, this is Miss Gracie MacDougal, Joseph MacDougal's daughter.'

There was a pause which lasted only a fraction of a second, but Gracie felt as if an electric current had passed between mother and son. 'Pleased to meet you, Mrs Cameron,' she said.

'Please—' the older woman smiled – 'Mary-Jane will do fine. It's the name of my business, and everyone in the district calls me that. I like it, it's friendly.'

She was pretty when she smiled. Gracie could see where James's dark-brown eyes had come from.

'And this is Mr Jones, Mother.' James had turned to Evan. 'He's – er—' He paused questioningly, unsure of the relationship.

Evan hastened to set matters straight.

'I'm a mechanic in Mr MacDougal's London garage. Mr MacDougal sent me to escort Miss Grace home because of the threatened rail strike.'

Mary-Jane's quick dark eyes took in the shining car parked outside the front window.

'Joseph's done well for himself.'

'Indeed he has, and I'm pleased for him,' Evan said warmly. 'We were prisoners of war together, you see.'

'Oh you poor souls! I didn't know.'

'After the war ended, Joseph contacted me and offered me this fine job which has many advantages, look you, such as obeying Miss Grace's slightest command.' He smiled.

They laughed and the atmosphere became more relaxed. 'Come and sit down.'

Their hostess led them through a wide archway into the living area of the large roomy kitchen. This had a dining table and assorted chairs, old, comfortable sofas dressed in flowery, faded chintz and armchairs grouped around a fireplace. A black and white cat luxuriated on a rag rug in front of the fire.

'Move over and let's see the fire, Brimstone,' Mary-Jane ordered. The cat rolled out of the way of invading feet, with a gleam of lazy green eyes and lash of bushy black tail.

'Tea, James, please. The kettle's boiling. Fruit cake in the tin.'

'Right you are!' He went off obediently while his mother seated the guests.

Watching James at work through the open archway, Gracie saw him prepare a tray with the same economical efficiency as his mother. She looked up to find Mary-Jane eyeing her thoughtfully.

'Did you know my father well?' Gracie smiled.

Did she imagine it, or was there the slightest hesitation before Mary-Jane replied?

'We went to the same school but in those days girls and boys did not mix. It was boys to the left, girls to the right. Joseph was a few classes above me and went on to grammar school. His young brother was in my class.'

'Miss MacDougal came to Kelso hoping to end the family feud, Mother.' James had been listening in the kitchen.

'Really?' Mary-Jane raised her eyebrows. 'Now there's bravery for you! Did you meet Angus MacDougal?'

'Yes, but when I told him who I was he shut the door.'

'He's a stubborn man!' Mary-Jane shook her head.

'I know. I only wanted a job.'

'You mean you aim to stay in the district?' She studied Gracie with heightened interest. 'What kind of job? In the house perhaps?'

'No, in the works.'

'The works?' She looked startled.

'You see, Mother.' James appeared with a laden tray which he set down on the table. 'This talented young lady

85

is an engineer. I knew you'd want to meet her before she went on her way.'

'Does she have to go, James?' the older woman asked.

'Of course she does. You heard her.'

Two pairs of dark brown eyes met. These two had no need of words, Gracie thought. Each seemed to know what the other was thinking. Without further ado, Mary-Jane dispensed tea and cake and the conversation became more general.

Gracie was eager to hear about the laundry business and their hostess was keen to explain. It soon became clear that Mary-Jane Cameron's laundry was an efficiently run enterprise, and her services much in demand.

'It must be hard work though,' Gracie remarked. She'd sampled the harsh realities of laundering when helping her mother at home and more recently during washday Mondays at Granton House.

'Yes, my dear, harder still when the weather's poor.' Mary-Jane took a sip of tea, carefully avoiding her son's eyes. 'Bella Brady next door helps out when she can, but I could do with extra help over the winter months. Would you be interested?'

'That's not a good idea, Mother!' James objected swiftly. '. . . er . . . I mean, Miss MacDougal wouldn't care to do that sort of work,' he added lamely.

Gracie considered the proposition. James was right in a way – the work did not appeal to her. In fact it seemed rather like scrambling out of hot water into the wash boiler, but on the other hand it would mean she could remain in the district and earn her keep while trying to break down her Uncle Angus's stubborn defences.

'Where would I stay though?' she said tentatively.

'Here, of course!' Mary-Jane smiled. 'I could deduct a small sum from your wages for board and lodgings. You'd be very welcome.'

'Ma, I told you. It's not a good idea!' James insisted.

'There's no harm in it, James.' His mother looked at him calmly. 'Angus MacDougal is a very stubborn man.'

'I know, but . . .' He eyed Gracie and fell unhappily silent.

Having met her dour uncle, Gracie could understand James's misgivings, but still she was tempted to accept Mary-Jane's offer. Foremost in her mind was the fact she needn't go back to London just yet to report failure and face dear Lady Frances's disappointment. True, the job meant more domestic drudgery, but it might lead to better things if she could wear down Angus's opposition.

The future began to appear a little rosier after all.

Watching her expressive features, Evan was alarmed. He did not trust these people. They appeared an honest, pleasant pair, but appearances could be deceptive. He'd learned that hard lesson in prison camp. Evan was sure mother and son had something to hide.

He'd watched them closely while sitting back and saying little. Now he detected an undercurrent of emotional excitement he mistrusted. He was afraid for Gracie, who didn't seem to notice anything out of the ordinary.

He drained his cup and stood up, making a play of glancing at his watch.

'Best to take more time to think about Mrs Cameron's offer, Grace. We should be on our way now.' He prayed she would take the hint but Gracie was in no mood to be dictated to.

'What's the hurry?' she frowned.

'Your father will be on his own and there's a deal of work waiting for me.'

'Then you go ahead, I'll stay.'

He groaned inwardly. He could see she'd made up her mind. Knowing Gracie, she wouldn't change it.

'That's settled then.' Mary-Jane rose to her feet, quick

and smiling. She put a hand on Evan's arm and he felt a gentle pressure hustle him to the doorway.

Looking down into dark brown eyes, he detected challenge. This woman was determined to keep Gracie in Kelso for reasons of her own. Why? To act as hard-worked labour – or for some other more sinister purpose? He glanced at Gracie, hoping she'd see sense, but she was relaxed and smiling.

'Tell Dad I'm learning how to run a small business while studying domestic science, Evan,' she laughed. 'Tell him I'll write to Lady Frances explaining everything.'

'Gracie, please—!'

The pressure on Evan's arm was firm and unrelenting. 'James, see Mr Jones out for me, will you, dear?' The little woman called to her son. 'I'll show Miss MacDougal her room.'

Evan gave in. There was nothing for it but to accompany James outside into the street.

'Nice car,' James said, examining the Sunbeam with a thoughtful look which Evan found disturbing.

Grimly, he handed out Gracie's baggage then climbed in and faced the young man.

'Remember I am not a man to be taking chances where Miss Grace is concerned, James Cameron!'

'Oh, that one knows her own mind.' He shrugged. 'Not much you can do about it, is there?'

'We shall see.'

Evan started the engine, and drove off without a backward glance. He had a plan in mind. What Gracie needed was a guardian angel, and he knew where to find one.

Outside Kelso, he took the Coldstream road and settled down to drive towards the Grantons' estate. He had recognized a while back that he and Sebastian Granton shared one passion in common, apart from racing cars, and that was Grace MacDougal. A word in Sebastian's ear, and

Evan was confident Grace would have an unlikely, but diligent, guardian angel.

Meanwhile, Gracie was inspecting the room Mary-Jane had assigned her. 'Oh, it's lovely!' she enthused.

And it was. The brass bedstead gleamed in late autumn sunlight streaming through white net screens. Sheets and pillowcases were crisp white, the patchwork eiderdown a soft blend of rainbow colours. The bedroom furniture shone with polish, and in one corner stood an ornate wash-hand basin with hot and cold brass taps, an unheard-of luxury which quite took Gracie's breath away.

Seeing her bemused expression, Mary-Jane laughed.

'James installed that, also the bathroom at the end of the corridor. My son's a very handy man!'

'Oh, he is!' she agreed fervently. She turned to her new employer, her face glowing. 'I don't know how to thank you, Mrs Cameron!'

'It's *Miss* Cameron, my dear,' the older woman said quietly.

'Oh . . . I'm so sorry . . .' Gracie stammered.

She thought the apology sounded inadequate, if not downright insulting.

Evan Jones was exhausted, his gammy leg aching as he pulled up at last in Granton Mews. He'd driven through the night, only snatching a couple of hour's rest by the side of the road. Joseph heard him arrive and came out of the garage wiping his hands. He frowned when he saw his mechanic was alone.

'Where's Gracie?'

'Still back home in your native land.' He climbed out stiffly and stood gingerly stretching his aching muscles while he told Joseph what had happened.

'For heaven's sake, Evan!' Joseph was not pleased. 'You know I didn't want her meddling with that family. You should've put your foot down. She's only a young lass after all.'

'With a will of tempered steel, like yourself.'

'Yes, well . . .' Joseph had experienced his daughter's iron will. He frowned. 'Who are these people she's taken up with?'

'A Mrs Cameron and her son. She's a washerwoman.'

'Cameron?' Joseph became still for a moment, then shook his head. 'It's a common enough name in that district. Did they seem decent folk?'

Evan hesitated. But what was the use of worrying Joseph with vague suspicions?

'Oh yes, indeed, they seemed very hospitable and decent,' he answered. He met Joseph's eye.

'And I took the precaution of alerting Sebastian Granton. He's to be in Scotland keeping an eye on the house till the estate is sold. He's promised to keep watch on Miss Grace too, and to bring her home kicking and screaming if need be.'

'Well done, lad!' Joseph MacDougal relaxed. He clapped his young friend on the shoulder. 'Master Sebastian wouldn't let any harm befall her. He has a soft spot for our Gracie. You know that, don't you?'

'Oh yes,' Evan said grimly. 'I know.'

'What an 'orrible day!' Rosie MacDougal complained, stamping icy feet in the beginnings of a puddle. 'It – it's just hell, Edwin!'

'Now, now! No offensive language, please.' He wagged a finger. 'Where's the sunny smile gone?'

'To blazes!'

Edwin considered her. She did look miserable. The red ribbon on the straw boater matched her nose, and beneath the green-striped overall, she was so bundled with jerseys and jackets you couldn't see how gorgeous her figure was.

Fortunately, the barrow was sheltered from the worst of the weather by other stalls selling clothing, china, books and so-called antiques, which to Rosie's jaundiced eye looked like old junk. The stalls were huddled together in a paved courtyard just behind the arcade, surrounded by two storey buildings, which at least tempered the searching east wind. Edwin had inspected the neighbouring stalls before setting up and had judged the goods on sale to be of a superior quality aimed at the up-town folk whose bus stop was nearby.

They'd done remarkably well, considering the awful day. The leather moneybag slung across Edwin's shoulder looked heavy. He picked out half a crown.

'Look,' he said. 'Why don't you give yourself a treat? Hop into DeMarco's over there and have a cupper and cream bun in the warm.'

'Edwin, I couldn't. That's a classy place!'

'Why not? You're a classy girl.'

'You think so?' She was astonished. She'd had nothing but cheek from him.

'Go on, the firm can stand it.' He pressed the silver coin into her cold palm.

'What about you?'

'I'm warm-blooded.' He grinned.

She took off the boater and apron and stowed them on the shelf under the barrow.

'I'll sit near the window so's I can keep an eye on the barrow. I'll be there in a jiff if you need me.'

'I know you will,' he said, and his tone was gentle.

DeMarco's was bliss. Seated at the window table, served by a deferential waitress, warmed by a generous pot of tea and pampered with a plate of assorted cream cakes, Rosie was in heaven. And there's plenty change from the two an' six, she thought, selecting a chocolate eclair to follow a cream bun.

She had a good view of the barrow from where she sat. It felt strange, watching Edwin at a distance instead of close up and aggravating. This was the way customers must view him.

He looked quite different. He was serving a customer at that moment, a glum-looking female under a black umbrella. In no time at all he had her laughing and smiling and was filling her shopping bag with brussel sprouts and an expensive bunch of exquisite black grapes. His final crack sent her away laughing happily, to catch the bus.

Rosie paused, the eclair halfway to her mouth. He was really charming in his funny, jokey way and exceptionally good at the job. And so good-looking!

Why didn't I notice before? she wondered.

Lily MacDougal had made a face when she stepped out into rain first thing that morning, but the weather hadn't dulled her bright expectations. This was her half day, the day she'd arranged to meet The Voice.

Lily was aware of dark clouds gathering all that morning as she sat at the switchboard, but she rather welcomed bad weather. It would be much cosier sitting in a tearoom at a table for two, rather than walking in a chilly park with yapping dogs, screaming children and curious passers-by as distractions.

Maybe he would choose an afternoon tea-dance, she thought with a lift of the heart. She'd put on high-heeled shoes and a swirly skirt that morning just in case they went dancing. The shoes were uncomfortable, but they made her look tall and elegant. Grandma Hawkins always said you must suffer to be beautiful.

Lily smiled. Could you fall in love with a voice? she wondered. Since they'd arranged to meet, the days had seemed endless, the fitful autumn sunlight brighter, the robin's challenging song sounded sweeter in the wind-blown air.

People had noticed, for Lily had bloomed too. Heads turned in the street as she passed and appreciative whistles followed her from young men. She didn't hear them. Her sparkling blue eyes, her thoughts, hopes and heart were firmly fastened on a dream.

Of course, there was another woman to contend with, a serious complication which somehow did not bother Lily in the slightest. In her job she had listened to many voices, and had decided that she trusted this one. Her sensitive ear had detected sincerity, honesty, gentleness, and most importantly for a young, fun-loving girl, a good sense of humour.

For the hundredth time she glanced impatiently at the crawling clock hands. She decided a tea-dance would be best, not too expensive in the afternoon either. The evening could take care of itself, but she thought she'd take him home and introduce him to the family. Yes, he had become that important to her!

But first, they would enjoy the shimmy, the foxtrot, the outrageous bunny-hug, might even have a go at a recent import from America, the Charleston, which was fast, furi-ous, rather daring and such fun! When her shift ended Lily nibbled a sandwich, drank a cup of milk in the rest room and quaked with nerves as the clock hands crept towards the appointed time. She settled her hat at a becoming angle, pulled on her gloves and headed for the main entrance.

'This came for you.' The doorman stopped her.

Wondering, she opened a little blue container which held a corsage of sweet-scented lilies.

'Oh, how thoughtful!' she gasped in delight.

'Pin them on your coat, miss,' the doorman urged. 'There, that's luverly. Don't you keep the young gent waiting now!'

She walked through the rain in a scented dream, hugging the knowledge that when she turned the corner she would see him, and he would know her because she was wearing his flowers.

She slowed as she reached the end of the street to calm her pounding heart, then took a deep breath to steady herself and went forward just as the church clock struck two.

She saw him at once, a tall rain-coated young man standing just inside the church's ornamental side gate. He'd been watching the corner, and when she appeared he snatched off his hat as if to fling it in the air for joy. Even at a distance across the busy street, Lily could feel the warmth of the smile which matched the voice. He set off, dangerously avoiding honking vehicles as he crossed over and came striding towards her.

'Lily! At last . . . !' He took her hand in his.

She heard the remembered voice, saw kind eyes, a humorous smile she would never forget, dark hair that curled and glistened with droplets of rain, the man of her dreams, but . . . but . . .

Dazedly, she took in the white dog collar, black clerical clothing beneath the raincoat. Visions of the tea-dance, the shimmy, the bunny-hug and the Charleston disappeared. You couldn't ask this man to go dancing. You couldn't laugh and flirt with him.

You couldn't fall in love with a clergyman! At least, a frivolous, pleasure-loving girl like Lily couldn't. It was quite impossible, and she couldn't hide her anguish and disappointment.

'Lily, what's wrong?' His smile faded.

'You talked to me in riddles.' She was close to tears. 'I asked if you were a singer or an actor, and you said you were a bit of both!'

'That's true.' He smiled faintly. 'You should see me

conducting the service in my East End church. They like sermons with a bit of drama and hymns sung loudly.'

'But you didn't tell me you were . . . you were . . .' She broke off. If she went on, she would break down and cry.

'A man of God?' he said gently. 'Oh, Lily, does it matter?'

'Of course it does!' she cried with a sudden wild burst of anger, pulling her hand away. She looked up into his face and the sweet scent of lilies drifted between them.

'Can't you see I'm not worthy of you?' she whispered brokenly.

Then she turned away from him, wobbling along in tottery high heels meant for dancing, running away from the man of her dreams before tears threatened to overwhelm her.

Polly MacDougal was at her wits' end. The beautiful daughters she loved with pride and deep devotion had become silent strangers. She didn't know what went on in their heads. All she had in answer to probing was yes, no and maybe from Rosie, silent misery from Lily and terse, scrappy notes from Grace, who was far away in Joseph's Scotland and working all hours of the day and night in a bloomin' laundry.

Joseph stubbornly refused to discuss Grace's behaviour and took a convenient wheezing fit if forced to talk about it. In desperation Polly would have confided in William Granton, but he had enough on his plate with business worries and strikes. That left Lady Frances, who was after all Gracie's employer and should be feeling aggrieved.

'Ma'am, I must apologize for my daughter,' Polly said.

'Oh, why?'

'She went off and left you in the lurch.'

'No, she didn't. Sebastian phoned to say the Scottish house is spotless from attic to cellar and Grace and Biddy

95

must have worked like Trojans, bless 'em. They deserve a break.'

'So Master Sebastian hasn't come home yet?' Polly looked grim.

'William asked him to supervise the sale. He'll stay in Scotland till everything's finalized. Don't worry, Polly, my son says he'll keep an eye on Grace.'

'It's not seemly for Master Sebastian to be spying on an innocent young girl!' said Polly truculently.

'Spying only in a manner of speaking, Polly.' Lady Frances smiled. 'Reading between the lines, Grace is thoroughly enjoying independence. There was a glowing account of life in the Borders in her last letter to me.'

'Letter? That's more than I've had!' Polly cried indignantly.

'Oh? I wonder why she hasn't written to you?' Lady Frances lifted her eyebrows.

Polly, struggling with a guilty conscience, could not find an answer.

Gracie had been working hard all week. A brisk, dry north wind had come whistling down from the Lammermuirs and driven Mary-Jane into a frenzy of washing.

The boilers began bubbling just after dawn most days and Gracie spent hours pegging out snow-white linen to flap on the lines, followed by long sessions on James's ironing board. Her pale London skin glowed rosily with the effects of fresh air and Mary-Jane's cooking. She was beginning to find her way around Kelso's cobbled streets, shopping basket on one arm. Heads turned and tongues wagged, but she welcomed that. She knew her presence in the district was bound to reach the MacDougals' ears. Surely her father's family couldn't continue to ignore her?

Sundays were a day of rest. As usual, one Sunday shortly after Gracie had arrived, Mary-Jane and Gracie dressed for church. As an afterthought, Gracie pinned the little motor car brooch Sebastian had given her to the lapel of her coat.

Her employer's quick brown eyes noted it at once.

'How unusual!' Mary-Jane laid a tentative finger on the lapel to examine the little car. 'Let me guess. It was a present from an admirer!'

'From a good friend, Mary-Jane.' Gracie laughed. 'Sebastian Granton gave it to me. They sell them in Woolworth's for sixpence, my sister says.'

'Oh, really?'

Mary-Jane assessed the value of fine rubies, emeralds, amethysts and diamonds set in gold. For future reference, she tucked away the information that the son of the wealthy Grantons from Coldstream was courting Joseph MacDougal's pretty daughter.

James Cameron came roaring into Kelso square on a motorcycle that afternoon. He balanced the impressive machine with both feet on the ground and shouted to Gracie.

'Care to come for a spin?'

Of course she couldn't resist it. She clambered onto the pillion, arranged her skirts more modestly, and they were off, Gracie's arms round the young man's waist.

Ignoring scandalized stares, James roared past the castle gates and headed out of town. To Gracie's alarm, their destination soon became clear.

When he reached the MacDougal works he turned in and stopped the bike. The silence seemed deep and ominous when the engine ceased.

'Oh, James! Why have you brought me here?' she cried in dismay. She wasn't prepared to tackle the MacDougals just yet. At least, not without a plan in mind.

'I wanted to explain something, that's why.' He helped her off the pillion.

The works were almost silent. the two or three men working that Sunday barely glanced up as James and Gracie went in.

Gracie looked round. It was everything she'd imagined it would be, an efficient, well-maintained engineering unit. James's latest tractor stood in a paint-spraying section at the back, bright-red and gleaming. 'The colour's a rebellion after the darkness and discomfort of war, and so is the comfort of a driver's cab,' he said proudly.

'If only my father could see this place!'

'He'd be kicking himself.' He laughed.

'James.' She turned to him. 'When we first met, you came from my uncle's house. So where do you fit in?'

'Well . . .' He hesitated. 'I suppose my mother's made no secret of the fact that I was born wrong side of the blanket. She's honest that way, but it's a severe disadvantage to a chap's prospects!' He sighed, then went on, 'I've worked my fingers to the bone for MacDougal's, breaking down prejudice and surmounting barriers, all in the hope of taking over when Angus retires. And now you come along!' He looked at her gravely. 'Pretty, winsome, and as it turns out, amazingly skilled and possessed of a full measure of MacDougal determination. I know fine you won't rest till you've wormed your way into Angus's heart, which is not so flinty as you might imagine. He never married, so he has no family and there are no heirs to carry on the business – till now.' He paused significantly.

'You're quite safe, silly!' Gracie smiled. 'Angus MacDougal can't stand the sight of me because of the stupid feud.'

'Ah, but there's the old lady, Angus's mother. I get on very well with the old dear and she likes me, but you might soften her heart and be in favour and I could be out of the running.'

'James, don't be daft.' She laughed. 'Your situation won't change just because I've appeared on the scene.'

'Oh, won't it?' His dark brown eyes were sombre. 'Your turning up has altered the state of affairs far more than you can imagine. Sometimes I curse myself. I should never have approached you that day, I should have let you go out of my life – but I was curious.'

'Curious? Why?'

He sighed.

'Because you're my sister, I suppose. Joseph MacDougal was my father.'

Six

S hocked, Gracie stared at James Cameron.

'You're my brother?'

'Half-brother, actually.' He looked grim. 'And I've been living with the consequences ever since. Mother keeps silent about my father, but makes no secret of the fact she's unmarried. She could make a pretence of respectability, but she's an honest soul and wouldn't dream of it. I think that's brave, Gracie.' He lifted his chin defiantly. 'Many folk don't see my existence in such a generous light, though. Life's been difficult – for both of us.'

'But my father's a good man, James!' Gracie was bewildered by these revelations. 'I can't believe he would abandon Mary-Jane when she was in trouble.'

'She didn't tell him.'

'Why not?'

'Don't ask me!' He shrugged. 'I gather Joseph had plenty to worry about at the time. She left home and went to live with a kind old aunt in Thurso in the far north of Scotland till after I was born.'

'What on earth had my father done?'

'I can't imagine.' James shook his head. 'But whatever it was, the MacDougals disowned him. He found a job with an English family soon after and went down south. My mother won't talk about him, and our mutual uncle Angus MacDougal doesn't know who my father was, of course. He'd never have taken me on if he'd known I was

Joseph's son. You found that out when he shut the door in your face.'

He stared moodily at the red tractor he'd designed with his knowledge of the wartime tank.

'You know, Gracie, my mother's an attractive woman and there have been men willing to take on a disgraced woman and her child. But she's rejected them all. I believe she still loves Joseph and will love him till the day she dies. Sad, isn't it?'

'I suppose so.' She sighed.

Privately, Gracie wondered how her kind, honourable father could have behaved so heartlessly, discarding poor Mary-Jane after all they'd been to one another. Maybe it was rough justice that he should have the son he'd always wanted and be unaware he existed.

A sudden thought struck her. What if her father found out about James and wanted to see him? How would her mother react?

Just then, a shadow darkened the doorway and Angus MacDougal stepped through the wicket gate. He glared at Gracie then turned his attention to James.

'How dare you bring women in here, Cameron!'

'Miss MacDougal says she's your niece, so I thought you wouldn't mind if I showed her round, Mr MacDougal.' James stood his ground. 'She says she's hoping you'll give her a job.'

'I've told her already we've no vacancies for women.' His expression darkened. 'As for you, miss—' he turned to Gracie – 'I'll thank you to get off my property this instant.'

'Surely not, sir!' James was hot with anger. 'I invited her in.'

'I know you did, my lad.' Angus said grimly. 'I saw your motorbike arrive with a female passenger and that set me wondering what you were up to. You've no right to bring unauthorized persons into the building outside business hours. I'll deal with you tomorrow morning in my office.'

'Don't you worry, Mr MacDougal, I'll be there!'

The two glowered at one another and with fresh insight, Gracie noted a strong family resemblance. Her own father was a mild-mannered man but had a stubborn streak and hot temper when roused. Just like these two. 'Come on, Gracie.' James grabbed her arm. 'Let's get out of here.' Their uncle followed, watching in dour silence as Gracie mounted the pillion. She glanced back over her shoulder as the motorbike reached the Kelso road. Angus MacDougal was still guarding the entrance to his engineering works like a dark sentinel, but somehow the solitary figure left Gracie with a strong impression of loneliness.

So why do I feel sorry for the grumpy old man? she wondered as the bike picked up speed and a stand of fir trees hid her uncle from view.

'We have a visitor, Gracie!' James shouted over one shoulder as they approached Mary-Jane's house. Gracie immediately recognized the car parked outside the door.

'Why, that's Sebastian!'

'What's Lady Granton's son doing here?'

'I can't imagine!'

Gracie was puzzled. How had Sebastian tracked her down? He was the last person she'd expected to see, considering they'd parted on such bad terms.

James brought the bike to a standstill and helped Gracie off. He looked down at her.

'What now, Gracie? Will you keep quiet about us, or will you spread the news?'

She hesitated. She had a new-found brother and wanted to shout it from the rooftops, but it wasn't so simple. Too many people might be hurt.

'No, James. We'll keep it to ourselves meantime.'

'That's wise.' He nodded agreement.

They found Sebastian seated on Mary-Jane's sofa balancing a teacup in one hand and a plate of cake in the other. He stood up politely when Gracie entered with James close behind.

'Ah, there you are, Gracie!'

'How on earth did you find me, Sebastian?'

'A little Welsh song-thrush told me.'

'Evan Jones!' she sighed. 'I might have guessed.'

James tightened his lips. So the Welshman had alerted Sebastian to act as bodyguard!

'I can see Mr Jones takes no chances where Miss MacDougal is concerned,' he remarked.

'Quite so,' Sebastian replied pleasantly.

Mary-Jane, dressed in Sunday best, sat opposite her visitor looking regal. She gave her son a reproachful glance. His tone had not been friendly.

'Mr Granton and I have had a nice chat, James.' She smiled at Sebastian. 'Your concern does you credit, Mr Granton, you must be busy attending to the sale of your parents' estate and Gracie should feel honoured you could spare the time to come and visit. You'll notice she wears your charming little brooch. So pretty and unusual!'

Her knowing smile told him she had assessed the value of the expensive jewel quite accurately. Was that probing little speech calculated to lay bare his intentions where Grace MacDougal was concerned? Gracie had taken a seat at the far end of the sofa and was watching him narrowly.

But Sebastian did not rise to his hostess's bait. 'I can always spare time to visit good friends, ma'am.' He smiled.

James poured a cup for Grace and held the teapot towards Sebastian. 'More tea?'

'No, thanks, but you go ahead, you must be thirsty after your trip.' He glanced out of the window. 'It's a magnificent bike. I'm quite envious.'

'Where did you take Gracie, James?' Mary-Jane's gaze rested icily on her son.

'To the works.'

'I thought so!'

'That's Gracie's family firm, isn't it?' Sebastian had detected a chill in the air, but was intrigued. 'I noticed the name on my way into town. I think I'll drop in and ask them to service my car. Maybe I should mention your father's garage in glowing terms, Gracie, tell them he's designed two racing cars and has plans for others. I bet they'll be impressed.'

Even Sebastian couldn't ignore the strained silence that greeted his innocent remarks. What on earth is going on here? he wondered, perplexed.

He finished the last bite of cake and stood up. His visit to the MacDougal family firm promised to be a most enlightening experience, he thought, as he shook his hostess's firm little hand and took his leave.

Joseph MacDougal had been nervy and unsettled since Evan Jones returned home without Gracie. As always when worried, his chest played up. He wakened in the night imagining he was back in prison camp, threshing around, unable to breathe. On those occasions he scared poor Polly out of her wits, quite convinced her husband was gasping his last. Joseph couldn't tell her the real reason for his distress . . . Cameron! A name from the past.

The name so casually mentioned by Evan Jones had awakened all sorts of emotions, buried deep. Yet goodness knows it was a common enough name in the Borders. Apart from giving Joseph the name and occupation of

Gracie's employer, a Mrs Cameron, Evan had provided no further details and Joseph had taken care not to show too much interest. But now he brooded constantly. Could the woman be related to Mary-Jane Cameron? Gracie's hastily scribbled postcards gave no clues, though he scanned them minutely.

Joseph had finally decided there could be no relationship between the two. He just couldn't imagine the well-off Mary-Jane he'd loved many years ago, related to a common washerwoman. Anyway, it still hurt Joseph to remember how shabbily Mary-Jane Cameron had treated him, abandoning him when he was in such dreadful trouble, leaving him to face disgrace – and worse – alone, when he had badly needed all her love and support.

No. This Mrs Cameron would be a poor widow making an honest living for herself. Which would explain why kind-hearted Gracie was helping her out over the winter months, having been sadly rejected by her own kith and kin. With a flash of indignant anger, Joseph recalled that his brother Angus had slammed the door in his sweet daughter's bonnie face.

He put a hand to his chest and took deep steadying breaths. Better not think along those lines or he'd be tempted to go and punch the man. Joseph left the office and made his way to the workshops. Things were quiet at the moment after a busy spell, and Evan was working on the racing car. He was a clever mechanic and had made several modifications to the engine's performance which Gracie and Sebastian would approve.

'With luck it will be finished when Miss Gracie comes home, Joseph.' Evan glanced up and smiled.

'Do you think she will? Come home, I mean?' In his blackest moods Joseph doubted if she'd ever come back now she'd tasted independence.

'Oh yes. I know it!' Evan was positive.

'I wish I could be sure!'

'Sebastian Granton will bring her back,' Evan declared confidently.

'He'll not leave Grace with people who do not value her. I'm thinking Mr Granton is a very determined man where Grace is concerned.' He studied the car he would mould into a winning machine for her dear sake. 'Almost as determined as I am myself,' he added softly.

That sunny November day, Rosie MacDougal had caught Edwin studying her covertly from behind the barrow.

'What you staring at?' she frowned.

'Your body.'

'Oh! How dare you!'

Edwin dodged the over-ripe tomato aimed at him and it splattered harmlessly in the gutter. He looked indignant.

'Arf a mo', Rosie, don't fly orf the handle. I didn't mean *that*. Anyway, you got more layers on you than a Spanish onion. No, I been reading an American book about marketing, and the chap what wrote it has been studying body language as an aid to selling.'

'Sounds creepy. You should stay away from that librarian woman you're so keen on. You haunt her bloomin' library every week.'

He ignored that jibe. He was studying her again, frowning.

'I mean, just look at you. You got your arms folded.'

'So what? I'm frozen stiff.'

'Rosie, Rosie!' He shook his head pityingly. 'Folded arms create a physical barrier between you and customers.'

'What you expect me to do – welcome Tom, Dick an' Harry with open arms?'

'Could be worth trying. We could charge extra.' He grinned, then caught sight of her wild expression and went on hastily, 'No, seriously, Rosie, we should cultivate a welcoming attitude if we're to open a shop.'

'Who said anything about opening a shop?'

'Oh, I mentioned the idea to Grandpa Hawkins.' He picked up a rosy apple and polished it on his apron, avoiding her eye. 'Good investment, a shop, specially if it's on a corner.'

'Edwin!' she exploded furiously. 'You may pull the wool over dear old Grandpa's eyes, but you can't fool me! Where's the money coming from?'

'Family capital and a bank loan,' he replied promptly. 'I already found out the rental of a nice shop I got me eye on and worked out a sensible sales plan for the banks to look at.' His eyes glowed eagerly. 'Imagine Hawkins enterprises concentrated in one big store, Rosie! We couldn't go wrong, girl. Any bank manager would jump at the chance.'

'Hit the ceiling, you mean!' she cried. 'Edwin, you'll ruin us! Hawkins have been hawkers ever since me great-great-granddad trundled a barrowload of apples into London down the Old Kent Road. We made our living off the barrows for generations. Hawkins don't know nothing else.' She was nearly in tears at the thought of him hoodwinking her beloved Grandpa and Grandma out of their life savings with smooth talk.

'That's history, dear girl.' He reached for her hand. 'You got to spend money to make money. Come on, Rosie, don't you think it's time for a change?'

'No, I don't!' She wrenched the hand away, then turned and ran into the arcade to sob out her bitter disillusionment on the comforting flower-scented bosom of dear old Grandma Hawkins.

Polly MacDougal was worried. Lady Frances was poorly, but it was not one of her usual attacks. This was a depression which seemed out of character and left the poor lady lacking energy to leave her bed. It seemed to Polly the illness had coincided with the arrival of the carter with an old battered trunk.

Master Sebastian had been clearing personal items from the Scottish house and had despatched the trunk, containing various treasured bits and pieces, to his London home. Lady Frances had ordered it brought to her room, and had begun rummaging through its contents.

Whatever unhealthy germ she'd encountered in there was the culprit, Polly decided.

She eyed the trunk with distaste as she brought in her lady's breakfast tray that morning. Pulling aside the curtains to let pale November sunshine creep in, she decided the ugly box sitting squarely in the beautiful room looked more menacing than ever this morning, if that were possible.

'Breakfast, my lady,' Polly said chirpily.

'I'm not sure I could manage any,' Lady Frances sighed wanly, her eyes fastened on that wretched trunk.

Something must be done!

'Shall I ask Percy to carry that old junk to the attic, ma'am?'

'No, no, Polly!' Lady Frances struggled up, quite agitated. 'There's something you should see, first.'

'Me, ma'am?'

She stared at the trunk apprehensively. The goods inside were packaged in straw and dusty wisps had escaped from the open lid. It had been a proper pest to Polly and the housemaid, who had spent hours picking up straw from carpets.

Lady Frances was watching her with a strange look that made Polly's heart miss an uncomfortable beat.

'Please look in the trunk, at the top,' she ordered.

Hesitantly, Polly parted a layer of straw and looked into

the box. There were toys further down, but on top lay a large leather book. A photograph album. She glanced questioningly at her mistress.

'Look at it.' Lady Frances commanded. Had Polly imagined it, or was there a hard edge to the voice?

With trembling fingers, Polly obeyed. She sank down on the daybed and slowly turned the pages. As she studied photographs of the early days of William and Frances Granton's marriage, her colour rose and she felt a rush of deepest shame.

Staring at the happy images of young love, Polly realized that the love she'd imagined Sir William had for her was only an illusion, a passing fancy with little depth. Oh, he'd sworn he loved Polly and maybe he did in a way – but looking at these poignant photographs she saw now that he was just a sad and lonely man robbed of his beloved wife's company by a cruel illness. Frances would always be William's only true love.

Polly forced herself to turn the heart-breaking pages. They shed a shameful light on the harm she'd done to this loving couple while her own faithful Joseph languished in prison camp. No words could express her guilt as she gently closed the album.

Lady Frances was watching closely. Does she know about William and me? Polly wondered. She dared not look at her mistress. Her kind lady would see the tears, the shame, the sorrow.

'Thank you for opening me eyes, ma'am,' she whispered. She replaced the album reverently with the other mementoes of a life she could never share.

'You know, Polly dear, I believe I do feel hungry this morning!' Lady Frances smiled and lifted the silver dome off a helping of scrambled egg. 'Oh, and could you please ask Percy to take that old trunk to the attic now?'

Polly fled, barging into Sir William Granton on his way to bid his wife good morning.

'What on earth's the matter, Poll?' He steadied her.

'Nothing, sir.' Looking at him, she felt sickened.

'Is it Frances? Is she worse?' He grasped her arm. He'd been almost out of his mind with worry about his sick wife.

'No, sir. My lady seems much better.'

'Oh, thank God!' He sighed.

'Sir – if you'll excuse me—' She pushed past and scurried downstairs towards the servants' quarters.

Frowning, he watched her go. Something had upset Polly. Her sprightly humour and glowing health had always attracted him, but this morning she had looked pale and tragic. Had Frances said something to upset her?

Apprehensively, William opened the door.

His wife was sitting up in bed eating scrambled egg. At his approach, her face lit up and she held out a hand.

'My darling, I feel better!'

'What a relief!' He sat beside her. 'I can't concentrate when you're ill. I let the business go to pot, sweetheart.'

'I know.'

She knew him so well, this man she loved with all her heart. She knew his strengths – and freely forgave his weaknesses.

'I met Polly outside. She seemed – er – harrassed,' William ventured.

'Oh, you know how fussy and tidy dear Polly is.' She laughed. 'That ugly old trunk of Sebastian's has been driving her up the wall. I finally gave permission to consign it to the attic. I expect she was rushing off to fetch Percy before I change my mind again.'

'Ah. I see!'

He glanced thoughtfully at the trunk. He'd looked through it himself and knew it held Sebastian's treasured old toys mostly, but more significantly it also contained their honeymoon album. He knew it gave a very revealing glimpse of devotion and happiness in the early years of their marriage before illness struck. William could imagine Polly's reaction if she ever saw it.

Did Frances suspect that he had strayed? he wondered. He had adored Frances from the first moment he met her and would love her devotedly till the end of his days, but that did not blind William to certain aspects of her character. She loved pulling strings. William suspected his wife had contrived to send Polly's daughter to Scotland, and had sent Sebastian racing after, to keep an eye on the young girl. It would be in character for Frances to make sure that Polly saw those poignant photographs.

Lady Frances finished breakfast and lay back against the pillows with a contented sigh.

'I feel much stronger. I think I'll get up today, darling.' She laughed teasingly. 'You can go to the office and concentrate on business with an easy mind, William dear.'

He leaned across and kissed the beautiful rascal tenderly. He was convinced that Polly MacDougal had seen that album. Frances had made sure of it.

Thank heavens Polly had made him see sense when Joseph returned home! William thought thankfully. Now, finally, the clandestine affair was over.

Lily MacDougal had lost her sparkle, though fortunately nobody had noticed. Her family were preoccupied with their own worries, and of course the switchboard at the London Exchange was a constant babble of frantic activity in December. None of her friends had a moment to spare. Lack of sparkle didn't show on the outside anyway. It was a secret loss inside.

The Voice hadn't contacted her since their disastrous

meeting. Quite honestly, she couldn't blame him. A vicar, and a flightly girl like me! Lily thought miserably.

She cringed every time she remembered the meeting. Fancy going to meet a man of God wearing high-heeled shoes meant for dancing, with a head filled with thoughts of the Hammersmith Palais, the foxtrot, tango and – heaven help us! – the scandalous bunny-hug.

And yet . . . and yet . . .

She couldn't forget him. Every detail of his appearance remained crystal clear, but especially the look in his eyes when he said her name.

'Lily! At last . . . !'

She didn't know his. The encounter hadn't lasted long enough for a formal introduction and she was glad of it. A name would have given him identity and substance, and she felt safer without it.

As days became weeks it became obvious he didn't intend to contact her, and Lily set about trying to forget.

She threw herself into a wild Christmas season of dating and flirting. She danced till all hours on Saturday nights and made eyes at all the bedazzled men who asked her out. She cropped her fair hair and wore short black evening gowns that glimmered with jet-black beads and showed off her shapely legs nearly to the knee.

She outlined her eyes with black mascara and her lips with scarlet and experimented with quick, unsatisfactory kisses that left her unmoved.

Her slim wrists jangled with cheap bracelets and her white throat was ringed with ropes of imitation pearls. She glowed, shone and glittered when on the dance floor. Other dancers paused to watch.

But only Lily knew the sparkle had gone.

Mondays were awful. She dragged herself to work after hectic late nights and sat all day at the switchboard with a voice grown husky and dull from hours spent in smoky atmospheres.

She knew there was no smile in her voice now. But what do I care? she thought. He will never phone me again.

The last Monday before Christmas, once work was over, Lily jammed a black pudding-basin hat over her cropped hair and shrugged on her oldest coat, a shabby brown thing whose only virtue was rain-proof warmth. She wound a black scarf round her throat, buttoned her feet into rubber galoshes and went out into a damp foggy night.

There was a man leaning against the doorway, finding shelter from the biting cold. Lily prepared to hurry past, for there were plenty of pitiful beggars in London these days, mostly old soldiers down on their luck. It broke her heart to see them.

To her dismay, this one put out a hand and stopped her.

'Lily, please wait . . . !'

'You!' It was the voice she could never forget.

He looked different. At first she couldn't say why, because her eyes were drawn to his face, shadowed by a jaunty trilby. Then she noticed he wore an ordinary shirt and tie, a grey overcoat covering a pin-stripe suit.

'You see?' His eyes twinkled with a hint of mischief. 'I'm incognito tonight. I didn't want to scare you off a second time.'

'You never phoned!' It was the first thought that came into her head, and with sudden insight she knew it was the reason for weeks of misery.

'I agonized about whether to contact you, then decided you must have time to adjust to what I do. I'm sorry, Lily. I should've warned you I was a preacher, but look!' He spread his arms. 'Today I'm just one of the crowd.'

At that moment, women from Lily's shift came running down the steps muffled in winter clothing, and she

113

smiled. She too was one of the crowd, her nose red as a cherry, looking far from her best in old clothes and galoshes. She was glad he was seeing her like this. This was the real Lily, not the gilded Lily of the dance floor.

'And I don't even know your name,' she said.

'We never got around to introducing ourselves, did we?' he said with surprise. 'I'm Matthew Mark Peterson.'

'And I'm Lily Hawkins MacDougal.'

'Shouldn't we say how d'you do and pleased to meet you?'

She laughed as they solemnly shook hands, the first real laughter for weeks.

'Do you have time to spare? Will you come with me?' he asked, suddenly serious.

'Yes – of course.'

He tucked her hand under his elbow and set off down the road.

'Where are we going?' she asked. They had left brightly lit shops and streets behind and were heading towards darker alleyways and lanes.

'Bright Street.'

'That sounds nice.'

'It isn't very nice – but the people are.'

'Is this your parish?'

'Yes,' he said shortly.

She stared at a black outline of old decaying buildings looming out of river mist in ill-lit streets near the docks. From here she could smell the cold oily smell of the Thames.

She clung more tightly to Matthew's arm and tried to suppress a shudder at the ugly chill of the place.

'So much needs to be done for those who live here, Lily.' He glanced down with a smile. 'Do you wonder I sometimes feel unworthy, too?'

'Evenin', Vicar.' A muffled figure loomed out of the darkness. 'Chilly, ain't it?' the man greeted him.

'So much for incognito!' Matthew laughed ruefully. 'Anyway, we've arrived. Here's St Agatha's.'

'Funny name for a church,' she remarked.

'The church is St Martin's-by-the-Marsh. St Agatha's is the soup kitchen.'

'You mean you have two saints?'

'Sort of. You see, Lily, my parents died in a house fire when I was small and I was brought up by Agatha Smithers, my mother's cook. A rather wonderful person. Agatha presides over St Martin's soup kitchen and has been granted an honorary sainthood by her customers.'

The surrounding air was succulent with the aroma of frying onions as he led her down an alleyway into a brightly lit hall filled with long tables and benches packed with gaunt men and women. Others stood patiently in a snakelike queue beside two steaming cauldrons and a massive copper tea-urn.

An elderly woman with a frizz of grey hair was doling out portions of soup and stew, sleeves rolled up to the elbows. A much younger woman filled mugs from the urn.

'Come and meet Agatha, our cook, and Marjory Carlisle, her second-in-command,' Matthew said, leading Lily forward.

'So that's where you got to, my lad! Took your time, didn't you?' Agatha eyed Lily thoughtfully.

'Never mind, Matt.' The younger woman laughed. 'You're just in time to help with the washing-up.' She sounded confident and happy as she teased him.

Lily, whose keen ear was familiar with most accents, recognized this one. The young lady from Manchester! She studied Matthew's Marjory with heightened interest.

Efficient, attractive and obviously dedicated to good

works, Lily thought as her spirits plummeted. She was suddenly aware of her own inadequacy in that direction.

Anyone could see that this smiling young lady from Manchester would be the perfect mate for the Reverend Matthew Peterson.

True to his word, Sebastian Granton made a point of visiting the MacDougal family business. He had to admit he was puzzled as he stopped the car in the forecourt and studied the place. Tidy buildings, impressive showroom. Why wasn't Gracie in here displaying her undoubted skills as an engineer, instead of up to her elbows in Mary-Jane Cameron's soapsuds?

He began to see why Evan Jones had viewed the Camerons, mother and son, with deep suspicion.

Sebastian walked boldly into the workshops and realized at once that this was no one-horse country blacksmith's, it was a sophisticated engineering unit with first-class equipment and, if he was not mistaken, an annexe at the back housing a drawing office. That indicated design, research and development of new models.

A red tractor caught his eye, with a cabin to shelter the hardy countryman who would drive it. There was a young man he recognized tinkering with the contraption.

Sebastian strolled over.

'So we meet again, James!'

'I've been expecting you.' James Cameron did not sound welcoming.

'Quite a spread Gracie's relatives have,' Sebastian remarked. 'It makes me wonder why her father is slaving away in London and Gracie is washing clothes for your charming mother.'

'You know how it is with families.' James shrugged.

'No, I don't. There's only me in mine. That's why I'm

interested in the MacDougals. When I was growing up, Gracie was like a little sister to me.'

'And what is Gracie to you, now she's grown up, Mr Granton?' James demanded. He had just discovered he had a young sister himself and felt protective.

'That's none of your damn business,' Sebastian frowned. He did not care for the man's tone.

He discovered he shared Evan Jones's uneasiness about this pair. First the mother wanted to know Sebastian's intentions where Grace was concerned and now the son had turned insolent.

Where, Sebastian wondered, did Gracie fit in?

'My car's in the forecourt,' he said, hoping to lighten the mood. 'Are you going to attend to it, or not?'

'I advise you to try anywhere but MacDougals, Mr Granton,' James said earnestly. 'And by the by, stop visiting Grace. One courtesy call's enough. We're looking after her.'

'Oh, I know.' Sebastian retorted. 'That's what concerns me.'

'Now you listen here—' James began, angrily doubling his fists.

But Angus MacDougal had been watching the two young men from his office and had sensed trouble. Angus was keeping a strict eye upon James Cameron since he'd found him with Joseph's lassie. Only that morning he'd given the young man a piece of his mind and a stern warning. Cameron was a gifted engineer and Angus had his eye on him for promotion. He'd be reluctant to let him go, but wouldn't hesitate if he gave any more trouble.

'Is there a problem?' he demanded, appearing beside the two.

'Your mechanic seems reluctant to attend to my car.' Sebastian turned to the older man. 'I told him yesterday I was coming in and he made no objection then.'

'Are you one of Cameron's friends?' Angus asked in surprise.

'Not really.' Sebastian hesitated. 'But we do have a mutual friend – Miss Grace MacDougal – a relative of yours, I believe?'

'From the dim and distant past,' Angus admitted. Inwardly he was fuming. That persistent young minx kept cropping up! 'I'll tell the foreman to attend to your car.' He smiled at Sebastian. 'If you're interested in cars and engineering, why not look around the workshops till your car's ready?'

'Thanks, I'd like that.'

Angus turned to James, his eyes like ice.

'And I'll have a word with you in my office, Cameron, if you please.'

Gracie was pegging out washing that day. It was bitterly cold but clear and dry. A brisk wind tousled her hair and brought a rosy glow to her cheeks. It was a drying wind from the north and Mary-Jane maintained sheets were all the whiter for a touch of its freezing breath.

She could be right, Gracie thought as she admired the full clothes lines. The white linen flapped and billowed in the sunshine, dazzling her eyes.

She heard a familiar sound in the distance. Shading her eyes, she made out James's motorbike. He brought the machine to the front of the house and stopped the engine with a roar.

She frowned. He was home very early. Faithful to custom, he came striding round the back, dark hair windblown and expression alive with fury.

'James, what's happened?' He looked so wild she stepped back in alarm.

'I've been given the sack.' He pounded across the green to face her.

'Angus MacDougal and I had the devil of a row, and he told me to get out.'

'Oh, no!' She was horrified, knowing instinctively she was somehow to blame for the disaster. 'Won't he change his mind?'

'No, not Angus! I'm finished here, Gracie.' He looked down at her. 'But I know what to do. I'm off to London to see Joseph MacDougal. I'll ask my father to give me a job.'

Seven

'No, James.' Gracie's reaction was instant. 'That's not a good idea.' She could imagine the consternation there would be at home if James Cameron arrived in London claiming to be Joseph MacDougal's long-lost son. What on earth would her mother do?

'Why not?' He frowned.

'My dad doesn't know you exist. Mary-Jane didn't tell him.'

'I know . . .' James hesitated. 'But she did believe they'd be married one day.'

'Well, they weren't. He went off and found a job in London and married my mother instead. How will my poor mother feel if *you* turn up?'

'He should have told her years ago that he'd been in love with my mother and would have married her if the wretched family feud hadn't intervened.' James shrugged. 'Keeping secrets is dangerous. There's always a risk of being found out.'

Gracie could vouch for that. Hadn't she found out about her own mum and Sir William quite by accident? But she wasn't going to tell James about that.

'What about my sisters?' she argued. 'Rosie and Lily think the world of our dad.'

'*Our* sisters,' James reminded her. 'Sorry, Gracie, I can't put our father on a pedestal like you three do. Maybe it's time everyone faced the truth about him.'

The back door opened suddenly and Mary-Jane looked out.

'What's happened, James?' She had seen her son arrive home early and sensed trouble.

'MacDougal gave me the sack.' He crossed the grass towards her, Gracie at his heels.

'Oh James!' His mother paled. 'Why?'

'We had a row.' He shrugged.

'I warned you to watch your tongue, son!' The icy wind blew and she shivered. 'Better come inside before we freeze.'

Mary-Jane led the way through the steamy wash-house into the kitchen, pausing briefly to put a kettle on the hob. She then hurried through the wide archway into the sitting room and stirred the banked fire to a blaze. The cat, Brimstone, surprised by such unaccustomed luxury on a working afternoon, purred approval.

'I wish you'd kept your head, James,' Mary-Jane sighed, sinking into an armchair. 'Still, you're the head mechanic and MacDougal will find you hard to replace. I expect he'll take you back when he judges you've learned a lesson. Then if you play your cards right and keep in his good books, you could be managing director when Angus retires.'

'So I should be! I'm his nephew and Gracie's half-brother!'

Mary-Jane looked from her son to Gracie in dismay.

'You mean you've told her who your father was? Oh, James! Was that wise? I thought we'd agreed to keep that strictly to ourselves? You saw how Angus reacted with Gracie. If he finds out you're Joseph's son he'll never take you back on.'

'For heaven's sake, Mother!' James frowned. 'How could I keep quiet? I've just found out I have three half-sisters. I'm not an only child any more. I feel like

I've come in from a cold lonely billet to a warm house. Can you blame me for wanting to let Gracie know the truth?'

She sighed. 'No, dear, I suppose not.' Mary-Jane hesitated a moment. 'I never told you, James, but my parents wanted you adopted quietly by a Thurso family in the far north. When I refused, they disowned me and left Kelso in a hurry before I came back home with you, to shame them.'

'All this secrecy!' James exclaimed impatiently, 'What happens if I decide to go to London to meet my father?'

'You wouldn't!' Mary-Jane looked aghast at the thought.

'What else can I do? I'm not so confident Angus will take me back and I'm pretty sure my father will give me a job if he knows who I am. You should be delighted!' he said with a trace of bitterness. 'London's a far cry from Kelso and you would be rid of an embarrassment.'

'Now listen, James!' Mary-Jane's brown eyes were bright with anger. 'I've planned and slaved for your future since the day you were born. When you showed promise as an engineer it was my ambition to see you at the head of MacDougals, where you belong. I believe there's still hope despite today's upset. But not if you go running to Joseph MacDougal in London.' She leaned forward, clutching his arm. 'If you do and Angus gets wind of it, you're finished. Like your father before you, you need never come back to Kelso.'

'I can't believe this!' He shook her hand off and stood up incredulously. 'You brought me up in an atmosphere of intrigue that's blighted my whole life, and now you tell me I must not meet my own father and sisters! Well, Mother, I'm a grown man. You can't tell me what to do and you can't threaten me. I'll go my own way and if that means you and I can never meet again, then so be it!'

Mary-Jane stared at her son and slowly her eyes filled

with tears. Gracie couldn't believe it. Mary-Jane, the strong, the unemotional, weeping!

'Ah, don't—!' James made a move towards his mother, then stopped. 'I'm sorry, Ma,' he said sadly. 'Maybe we're too much alike, you and I. You were never afraid to face the consequences of your actions, were you?'

She wiped her eyes. 'No, son, never!'

He gave her a quick, awkward hug. 'Aye well, I only hope I can be so brave.'

With that, James left the room.

The two women listened to his footsteps in the hallway and heard the front door close behind him. The motorbike engine roared, then puttered off down the street to be lost eventually in a forbidding silence.

'Oh, Mary-Jane! What will he do?' Gracie asked.

'What James always does when troubled, my dear.' Mary-Jane sighed. She blew her nose and sat up, in command of her emotions again. 'He'll go to the shed where he stores the motorbike and overhaul that wretched machine down to the last nut and bolt.'

'Yes, of course.' Gracie nodded with relief. In times of stress she'd resorted to that healing procedure herself.

'We'll be lucky if he turns up before midnight,' his mother said. 'But I wish I knew if he's preparing that bike for a long trip to London or a short trip along the road to apologize.'

The kettle boiled. Gracie rose quietly and went through to the kitchen to brew a pot of tea. She was sure they both needed it.

Gracie slept fitfully that night and heard James come home very late. When she hurried down to breakfast at seven, he'd gone.

'Not to London,' Mary-Jane said thankfully, dishing out porridge. 'He was wearing old working breeks and overalls and took a set of spanners with him. Signs are he's still working on the blessed bike.'

After she'd finished breakfast and washed up, Gracie decided she couldn't let matters drift. Some drastic action must be taken. It was another cold blustery day and Bella from down the road had come in at Mary-Jane's request to tackle heavier items of laundry. Gracie's presence was not required in the wash-house with Bella in command. Mary-Jane withdrew to the office to make out invoices, and barely lifted her head when Gracie looked in to say she was off on a shopping trip.

Studying herself in the mirror, Gracie was pleased with the reflection. She had dressed with care. Her hat was smart but not too fancy. Coat, gloves and scarf were in the best of discreet taste, shoes polished to a shine. She decided she looked business-like, but quite appealing. Quietly, she let herself out of the house and headed for the bus stop in the centre of town.

Sitting in a bus heading along the road which passed MacDougal's works, Gracie's courage began to fail. What did she think she was doing, interfering in these people's lives once more? They were family, but they didn't want to know her.

What did she hope to achieve? To charm Angus MacDougal into giving James his job back? Oh Gracie! What a hope! As the works buildings came in sight, she hesitated, then stood up on shaky legs.

'Oh, so it's you again!' Angus MacDougal growled when the receptionist showed her into his office.

'Yes, Mr MacDougal,' she said bravely. 'But this time I've come to apologize. I'm very sorry I tried to meddle in family matters I don't understand. It was silly of me.'

'So it was.' He nodded more agreeably.

She was encouraged to go on.

'So I came to tell you I've decided to leave Kelso and go back to London and leave you in peace.'

'I thought you'd planned to work a winter in Cameron's laundry?' He raised his brows.

'So I had, but I can't stay on now you've given James Cameron the sack because of me, can I?'

'Not because of you, Miss MacDougal,' he corrected her. 'I can't altogether blame a man for being led astray by a pretty face, but Cameron insulted me. I had to let him go.'

'But he's a gifted engineer! Oh, Mr MacDougal, I feel so guilty. I cost him his job. If James apologizes and promises to behave in future, won't you please take him back?'

Angus MacDougal studied her thoughtfully.

'Sorry lass, I can't. The job's not available any more. I've found someone to replace him.'

Gracie was speechless. She'd been prepared for argument, but not for this final blow.

'If you'll just come with me for a moment, miss?' He came from behind the desk and stood beside her. There was nothing for it but to follow her uncle.

Angus MacDougal led the way through large engine sheds where men were working and into a smaller space which reminded Gracie poignantly of her father's cosy workshop in the mews. Nostalgically, Gracie breathed in the evocative smell of grease, engine oil and petrol which lingered about this area. Looking beyond a big table covered in blueprints, she noted with interest the skeleton of a motor car set up on jigs.

A man in overalls was down on one knee tinkering with the rear axle. Aware of a presence, he glanced up and grinned.

'Hi, Gracie! I hoped you'd show up soon.'

'Sebastian!' she gasped.

Sir William Granton's son and heir rose and strolled across, wiping oily hands on a rag.

'Welcome to my new job, old girl. I came in to have my car serviced and Mr MacDougal kindly showed me the firm's latest venture.' He waved a hand towards the skeletal structure. 'I suggested some improvements that impressed him and here I am. Luckily for me, there was a vacancy.'

'But what about the sale of your parents' estate?'

'All in the auctioneer's hands,' he assured her. 'But since I've finished my degree and there's no place for me in the London office at present, the Old Man suggested I stay in the district for a spell to make sure tenants and employees are treated fairly and suitably re-housed where necessary.'

'Why must you work here?' she wailed.

'I have to find a job somewhere, of course, or I'll die of boredom. This one suits me far better than office work. I've promised Mr MacDougal if he finds my work is satisfactory I'll stay till this motor is on the road.' He turned his attention to the car. 'It's rather a wonderful concept, Gracie. This car will take steep hills and muddy tracks in its stride just like a tank! I've studied the blueprints, and the gearbox is quite amazing. Pity we couldn't work on it together, old girl. It'll be larger and heavier, but maybe we could introduce the modifications we built into the racing car your father designed, to lighten the chassis.'

As always, Sebastian's enthusiasm was highly infectious. How Gracie longed to agree! It would be wonderful to work with Sebastian again upon such a revolutionary new project.

But she knew it was impossible. There was James Cameron's future to be considered, and there was her uncle's ominous presence standing by, watching her dourly . . .

*   *   *

126

Grandpa Hawkins had never heard such a dog bite and bow-wow! The row was taking place in the arcade after hours – fortunately empty of customers and traders at this time of night. In fact, there had never been such a flaming row in the Hawkins family that Grandpa could recall. But then of course there had never been such an ambitious proposal put to the Hawkinses before.

A shop. Blimey!

Grandpa had whipped the green cloth off the counter when he called the board meeting and he now prepared to hammer on wood in a bid to prevent his granddaughter Rosie and Sid's stepson from murdering one other.

'A bank loan?' Rosie was bellowing. 'You gone mad, Edwin? Hawkins never have debts, not even a ha'penny!'

'I didn't say debts, I said capital!' Edwin yelled just as fiercely. 'Might as well forget about making a fortune if you don't have capital to start off with. I got a bank loan lined up.'

'Your bank manager must be barmy!'

'He knows we have assets, Rosie. Me ma's house is worth a packet and she's offered it to Sid as collateral.'

'Well, I'll eat me bloomin' boater!' Rosie gasped. 'You hear that, Grandpa? He'd ruin his poor old ma without turning a hair and spoiling his brilliantine!'

'Now, 'arf a mo, Rosie girl.' Grandpa Hawkins raised a hand. 'If your Uncle Sid and his missus are willing to back the boy with hearth and home, that's saying something in my book. Me and Grandma have a bit put by. We could chip in.'

'You and Ma wouldn't lose out, Dad,' Sid broke in, beaming proudly on his stepson. 'Edwin's bright. Edwin's going places.'

'Whoahh! Stop right there!' Rosie cried.

127

It had the desired effect. They stared in silence while she held the floor.

'Now I don't deny Edwin's bright,' she went on grudgingly, 'but Edwin's on barrows like the rest of us. He don't know nothing about running shops. If he tries that caper, I reckon the only place Edwin's going is down the drain, and our money goes with him. You'd be daft to trust 'im.'

Edwin had turned deathly pale. Rosie had never seen him so white, just as if he was frozen in a block of ice. For a moment she thought he'd had a heart attack, then he seemed to leap back to life, the ice melted by a fiery inner glow.

'Fair enough. You had your say, Rosie. Now it's my turn.' Grimly, he turned his back on her and addressed the rest of them. 'Rosie's right, I don't know nuthin' much about running a shop,' he admitted candidly, then dropped his voice to a persuasive pitch, '—but I do know goods sell best on a corner site on the busiest side of a busy street. I know people expect high standards but don't want to pay through the nose. I know East Enders appreciate a smile, a bit of special attention, a joke and a laugh. I know I can sell cheap what people want at prices that won't ruin us.' He paused, and produced a trump card. 'Old Jesse Boot filled the windows of 'is chemist shop in Nottingham with packets of Epsom Salts going cheap. Sold like 'ot cakes, they did, and just you look at Boot's stores today!'

Edwin glanced round a circle of rapt faces. He had the meeting eating out of his hand – except for one. He met Rosie's eyes. 'It only took faith from 'is family and 'ard graft from old Jesse Boot to build an empire. Why shouldn't Hawkins do similar?'

Sid clapped loudly at the end of his stepson's impassioned speech.

Grandpa rapped sternly on the board. 'Meeting will come to order!' He scribbled on a notepad for several

128

seconds with the pencil kept stowed habitually behind one ear. 'Noted in the minutes that Hawkins family trustees considered Edwin Barlow's proposal to open a corner shop.' Grandpa looked up, spectacles perched on the end of his nose. 'We've 'ad debate and 'eard arguments, ladies an' gents, now all that's needed is a show of 'ands. Those in favour –'

Grandpa raised an arm, so did Sid, Rosie folded her arms, Edwin was ineligible, so all eyes turned to Grandma, who hadn't said a word so far.

Grandma had the casting vote.

Rosie held her breath. Surely Grandma wouldn't sacrifice a comfortable retirement for Edwin's shopping empire in the sky? Grandma Hawkins gave Rosie a special loving look that caused her granddaughter's heart to lift hopefully.

'Now we all knows our Rosie's a chip off the old Hawkins' block!' Grandma Hawkins smiled. There were murmurs of approval. 'What Rosie says carries weight.' She went on. 'We knows the old barrows are tried and tested and have given us Hawkins a good living for generations. Me and Grandpa worked in the East End on barrows all our lives. We've been luckier than most, mind. Our Polly and our Sid done well for themselves, and so they should, for we always lived decent and respectable, kept clean when it wasn't easy to do and played fair with customers. We had faith in the future, see?'

Heads nodded agreement. Grandma continued. 'Now – to my way of thinking, Edwin Barlow is the future. If the boy thinks a corner shop is the way forward, he could be right. 'Sides, I can see us doing East Enders some good in these 'ard times if we has a shop. Maybe 'elp the jobless who've not much more'n a Relief Ticket to feed a family. So I'll show me 'and and back the boy.' Solemnly, Grandma raised an arm.

Chilled to the bone, Rosie stared at her grandmother. There was a long uncomfortable silence, broken only by odd, creepy echoes that murmured through the empty arcade at night.

'Motion carried, Rosie! Sorry, girl,' Grandpa declared heavily.

'Formal notice to the Chairman, Grandpa.' Rosie raised her chin. 'You can write down in the minutes that Miss Rosie MacDougal gives notice of her resignation from the board forthwith, this action to be confirmed in writing in due course.'

'Aww, Rosie! Aww, girl!' He looked stricken. They all did.

Rosie paid no heed. She flung the straw boater with the jaunty red ribbons down on the board and walked out into the cold.

'Not going to church?' Polly MacDougal gasped, staring at her daughter Lily in horror.

Polly rarely missed Sunday worship. She loved St Bartholemew's-in-the-Park, the beautiful little church situated close to Granton Mews. It stood at the end of a quiet avenue lined with glorious lime trees whose fresh young leaves were a wonderful shade of green in springtime. A delicate spire pointed heavenwards and uplifting stained-glass windows donated by past generations of Grantons cast rainbow colours over carved pews.

Ever since early days as Lady Frances's personal maid, it had given Polly immense satisfaction to walk up the wide front steps accompanied by her three pretty little daughters, to take her seat modestly in a pew just behind her employers. It was such a beautiful clean church and lovely smart congregation, compared with the East End Mission Hall and rag-tag assembly of Polly's childhood. That was a gloomily soot-stained and unlovely building which her parents had attended faithfully and supported loyally.

Polly had never persuaded her husband to accompany her to church. Even their simple wedding ceremony had taken place in a bare room behind the Mission Hall. Joseph would never explain why he wouldn't go. He was well brought up, well-educated, and why he persisted in behaving like a heathen remained a complete mystery to Polly.

And now this Sunday, to Polly's consternation, here was her daughter Lily showing similar signs of rebellion.

'I didn't say I *wasn't* going to church,' Lily said, her cheeks pinker than usual. 'I'm visiting *another* church, Mum.'

'I bet you're going with a fellow!' Polly was suspicious. 'Come on, Lil, come clean. Is it someone unsuitable?'

'Of course not!'

But her mother was a little too close to truth for comfort. The Reverend Matthew Peterson had walked Lily home to Granton Mews after her visit to the East End soup-kitchen that memorable evening. They hadn't spoken much on the way, but Lily had found silence more exciting than idle chat. She could remember every emotion she'd experienced on that magical walk with him by her side through dark wet streets, rubbing shoulders with gaunt men and shawled women who'd greeted Matthew like a friend. She had only to close her eyes and she was there again.

She remembered a trolleybus had startled her as they'd prepared to cross the road. It had clanged past so close she'd seen sparks fly from overhead wires, blue and brilliant in the wet night. He'd pulled her back from the kerb, then they'd crossed the road together, his arm around her. It had seemed as if she floated. She couldn't remember her feet touching the ground.

She hadn't asked him in and he had made no move to kiss her in the shadow of the archway where she'd slapped the face of more than one amorous dance partner in the wild dancing days. She couldn't recall what he'd said on parting, except that he'd made no mention of seeing her again. All she could remember was how cold the rain had felt and how dismal the night had seemed after she had watched him walk away.

'Well, you're up to something.' Polly gave the smart blue hat Lady Frances had handed down to her an exasperated tweak. 'You can't fool me, Lily MacDougal.'

'If you must know,' Lily sniffed, 'I'm going to church with Marjory Carlisle, one of my girl friends, Mum. She helps out in a soup-kitchen beside the church afterwards, and I promised I'd give her a hand.' Lily's explanation did hold a grain of truth. Marjory was kind and caring and the friendly smile she'd given Lily when they'd parted in the soup-kitchen had seemed genuine enough.

'You'll come again, won't you, Lily? We could do with another pair of hands,' she'd said.

Lily had eyed her suspiciously, aware of her own limitations as cook and dishwasher, wondering if Miss Carlisle intended making a fool of her. But Marjory's eyes were innocent and her expression guileless. Lily had mumbled a promise, and felt humbled and shamed.

That had been two or three weeks ago and to be honest she wasn't sure what invisible force was pulling her back to St Martin's this Sunday morning. Marjory would be unfailingly kind, but Matthew would be delivering a sermon and would probably ignore Lily's presence altogether. He would probably think it was cheek on her part, barging in uninvited.

'You better have a good scrub in the bathtub with Lifebuoy soap after mixing with that dirty lot,' Polly warned darkly. In Polly's opinion, Grandpa and Grandma Hawkins did more than enough for poor hungry souls in the East End, without Lily's well-off girl friend muscling in when the pair of them should be out finding husbands. I mean, look at our Rosie! Polly grumbled to herself. Rosie looked nothing but glum these days, and no wonder. No sign of a steady boyfriend there!

Of course, there was a sad and terrible shortage – a whole generation of fine young men lost forever in the fields of France.

If Lily had hoped to recreate the magic of that rainy night, she was sadly disappointed. Bright Street that Sunday morning was anything but bright. The houses were built of soot-blackened brick roofed with mossy broken slates pierced by precarious chimney stacks. Two featureless terraces bordered a narrow street terminating in padlocked dock gates. Yet Lily noted scrubbed doorsteps and bravely whitewashed window sills amongst the dilapidation. The sight touched a sympathetic chord. But when she reached Matthew's church, she saw that in far-off days when Bright Street was a pathway to the sparkling river, St Martin's-by-the-Marsh must have been beautiful. It sat in its own paved courtyard sheltered by the stone walls of the church hall dedicated to Matthew's St Agatha – the stalwart woman who'd brought him up. Behind, lay an ominous gap where bombs had fallen, destroying houses and neatly shearing off the topmost third of the church spire.

Lily joined a crowd heading into church. She had taken care to dress in her oldest clothes and simple beret, yet even so, she soon realized she was uncomfortably out of place.

Shining golden hair framed a lovely unlined face which invited envious stares from women grown old at thirty. Two or three little awestruck urchins timidly fingered the fine wool of her coat.

Inside, a noisy congregation packed the scuffed and battered pews. Babies wailed in mothers' arms and small children played tag in the aisles, a mongrel dog curled up beside one old man looked up at Lily with soulful

133

eyes and wagged its tail. She thought about the elegant congregation of St Bartholemew's in the park and couldn't believe her eyes.

'Lily!' Marjory Carlisle caught her by the arm just as she was retreating, having given up hope of ever finding a seat. 'How lovely to see you. Come and squeeze in beside us.'

'Is it always like this?' Lily asked in amazement when Marjory had seated her beside the comfortable bulk of Agatha Smithers, dressed in regal black velvet.

'Most Sundays,' Marjory nodded. 'Matthew swears it's the bowl of Agatha's broth afterwards that's the draw, but he's being modest of course.'

Her eyes were clear and candid and shone with a quiet inner confidence. Again, Lily was forced to question with a sinking heart Matthew's feelings for herself – surely Marjory was everything a man like Matthew would want in a wife?

There was a sudden hush as a door opened and Matthew ascended steps to the pulpit. An elderly woman began playing a wheezy harmonium that seemed to soothe babies and subdue children.

He lifted his head from an opening prayer – and noticed Lily. She didn't know how he could pick her out from such a multitude, but he did. He was smiling broadly when he stood up to begin the sermon.

'Consider the lilies of the field, how they grow . . . !'

His gaze sought Lily's and her heart soared to the high ceiling. But she watched compassionately as Marjory glanced up at Matthew in dismay, then down at her hands, suddenly clenched in her lap. So she loved him!

Lily wished she hadn't obeyed an overwhelming impulse to attend this service. She had no wish to complicate Matthew's courtship of this good young woman and upset Marjory with her presence here.

After the service Lily planned to slip away unnoticed,

but since it was Matthew's custom to have a word with everyone at the doorway he caught her as she tried to sneak past.

'Please wait, Lily. I want to speak to you.'

He smiled, and she had no choice but to stand aside and wait till the congregation had trooped into St Agatha's for the promised bowl of soup. They sat together in a rear pew of the empty church. Matthew seemed formal and unapproachable in the unfamiliar robes of his calling. Watching him, Lily felt nervous. He looked so serious.

'I've been offered the chance to join a church mission to Africa, Lily,' She was stunned. Congratulations seemed out of order, so she said nothing. 'They seem to think I could do some good out there, and help the people.'

Lily glanced slowly around the deserted church. She longed to say – but what about your own people? Don't they need your help desperately too? But the words wouldn't come.

'If I should agree to go they want me to recruit volunteers to teach in the mission school – preferably those with experience of the spoken word.' He looked at her steadily. 'Would you come to Africa with me, Lily?'

She wanted to tell him she would follow him to the ends of the earth, but she knew there was only one answer she could honestly give.

'No, Matthew. I'm sorry.'

'I thought as much,' he said quietly.

She wanted to reach out and take his hand, assure him she would always love and forgive him even though he had turned his back on poor East End folk who loved and trusted him.

But instead she stood up, said goodbye with a calm smile and left him standing in the doorway, watching her walk away down narrow, grubby streets blurred with tears.

At least he would not go alone to the mission in

sunny Africa, Lily knew. Marjory Carlisle would go with
Matthew Peterson without a second thought. Whereas Lily
– oh, how could she leave her beloved family and the life
she knew? It was too much to ask.

It's a long way from Kelso to London, especially on a
motorbike in early March. Despite oilskins and leathers,
James Cameron was frozen, wet and hungry when he
stopped for the night at a roadside inn. He was angry
too, which didn't help.

Although his chilled discomfort was soon eased by a
roaring fire and a large helping of beef steak pie, that did
not soothe a painful sense of injustice.

Gracie MacDougal had stolen James's job and possibly
his future! James cradled a welcome dram in his hands
and stared moodily into the flames. Strictly speaking, it
was Sir William Granton's son, Sebastian, who was the
culprit, but Gracie had charmed her way around Angus
MacDougal and was helping Sebastian build James's cherished car. Gracie of all people, his beautiful new-found
sister. What a betrayal! And she wouldn't even admit it
was a betrayal!

During the row they'd had after she'd confessed what
she'd done, Gracie had justified treachery with femin-
ine logic.

'Surely you can see I'm only working in MacDougal's
on your behalf, James?' she'd cried as they stood glaring
at one another in his mother's sitting room. Mary-Jane had
been present too, but grimly silent.

'How d'you work that out?' he'd demanded.

'Sebastian's a fine mechanic, but he won't stay in Kelso
once the new car's on the road. He can't. His father needs
him in the London office,' she had argued, then turned
on the charm. 'James, that car is going to be a winner.
Angus will be so pleased when orders come pouring in,

136

I'll persuade him to give you your job back. You designed the car, after all!'

'It'll take a few months yet to finish it. How can I twiddle my thumbs for months?'

'Take a temporary job with the blacksmith. You could man the petrol pump.'

He'd treated that suggestion with the scorn it deserved. Fortunately his mother had intervened.

'What about me, Gracie? You promised to help in the laundry, you know.'

'I'm sorry, Mary-Jane.' Gracie had the grace to look guilty. 'But when Angus said I could help Sebastian if I agreed to work for an apprentice's wage, I had to take the job. It's the only way I can help James.'

'Well, dear, in that case I suppose I could ask Bella to come in, though she's such a dreadful gossip,' Mary-Jane had sighed.

'Well, Bella will have plenty to gossip about,' James had interposed angrily. 'Because I'm leaving for London. Tomorrow!'

Sitting by the fire, James felt a twinge of guilt when he remembered how his mother had looked. She'd aged before his eyes, and become a lonely little woman facing yet another crisis her son had precipitated. His love for her had surfaced and he'd hugged her with an unusual display of emotion.

'I'll stay away six months, Mother,' he'd promised. 'Then I'll be back.' She'd looked at him with steady dark eyes that seemed to see into his soul.

'Will you really, James? I wonder!'

James sipped the whisky slowly. Now that he was not far from London and likely to meet his father very soon, who could tell what might happen?

James disliked on sight the vast, bewildering city of

London. The streets seemed narrower, more confined than those of his native Kelso, and much busier of course.

He soon discovered London traffic was not geared to motorbikes. The route James had chosen in ignorance led through areas congested by cars, taxis, buses and horse-drawn carts and it was late in the afternoon when he came to a weary stop outside his father's garage.

It was smaller than he'd expected. Accustomed to Mac-Dougal's engineering works, he'd imagined something grander. Already dampened, his spirits plummeted as he clambered stiffly off the bike and unstrapped the small case containing his wordly goods.

A man James recognized as the Welshman Evan Jones came limping out of the garage at that moment and confronted him. 'Do you know, when I heard a motorbike, Mr Cameron, my thoughts turned to you! Have you brought Gracie with you?' He couldn't hide his eagerness.

'No, I haven't,' James answered shortly.

'Why not?'

'Because the man *you* appointed as her bodyguard stole my job, and dear little Gracie is now working in the family firm, aiding and abetting the felony.'

'Sebastian? I can't believe it!' Evan looked startled by the news and somewhat distraught.

'It's the truth.' James shrugged. 'That's why I'm here. The MacDougals owe me a job.'

'I suppose you had better come inside.' Evan looked uncertain for a moment. 'Joseph will want to hear news of Gracie.' He led the way into the garage.

James glanced around with a critical eye but couldn't fault the workshop. It was well-equipped and much larger than he'd suspected from outside. The Welshman opened a door leading into a small office and glanced in. There was an older man working with T-square and set square at a desk and James's heartbeat raced, very close to panic.

He was about to meet his father at last.

Eight

Joseph MacDougal couldn't hide his eagerness when Evan ushered James Cameron into his office.

'You'll have brought our Gracie with you, Mr Cameron?'

'No sir, I'm sorry. I tried to persuade her to come with me, of course, but Gracie had other plans.'

'Plans? What plans?' Joseph was bitterly disappointed. He glared at James indignantly. 'Look here, Cameron, I was assured Gracie would be working in Scotland for a fortnight at the most, and now it's been nearly three months. Last time I heard she was working in a laundry helping your mother. So what's going on?'

'Mr Cameron says that Gracie is with Sebastian Granton,' Evan interrupted.

'What?' Joseph was outraged. He turned to James. 'Is this true?'

'Yes.' The younger man nodded nervously. 'They're working together at MacDougal's works, building a motor car. It's a new model your brother hopes will be a winner in Scotland, Mr MacDougal. You see,' he went on more confidently, 'I was head mechanic at the works till Mr Angus dismissed me and gave the job to Sebastian. Then he took Gracie on as apprentice.'

'But I thought my brother would have nothing to do with her?' Joseph frowned.

'He must've changed his mind.' A hint of bitterness crept into James's voice. 'Gracie can be very persuasive.'

140

'That's true, Joseph,' Evan nodded agreement. 'It can be difficult to resist Gracie's charms when she sets her heart on something.'

Joseph eyed James with suspicion.

'Why did *you* get the sack?'

'I told Angus MacDougal what I thought of him and his family.' James's eyes flashed angrily.

'I'm a member of that family too, mind!' But the heat had gone out of Joseph's tone. This astute young man had obviously taken his brother's measure.

'What brings you here anyway?' he asked curiously.

James met his father's eyes, which were disturbingly like Angus's. He hesitated. Should he reveal the relationship? Maybe not when emotions were running high. Perhaps this was not the right moment.

'I reckon the MacDougals owe me a job,' he said boldly.

'Oh, you do, do you?' Joseph studied James without much enthusiasm, then glanced at the Welshman. 'What d'you think, Evan? Could we do with an extra hand?'

Evan hesitated. He had not trusted James Cameron when he met him in Kelso, and saw no reason to trust him now. But that did not answer the question. With more cars on the road and Joseph subject to bouts of ill health, Evan could barely cope with the extra work. James Cameron could be a godsend.

'There is no doubt we need help, Joseph,' he admitted.

'I suppose I needn't hope for glowing references?' Joseph looked at James. 'I thought as much! Well, I'll pay the going rate, and there's a small furnished flat over the old coach-house you can have rent-free. And I reserve the right to dismiss you without notice if your work's not up to scratch. Agreed?' He fixed the young man with a stern gaze.

Once formalities were completed, Joseph relaxed and smiled at his new employee.

'Well now, you've had a long, cold journey today, James, and I know my wife would be delighted if you and Evan would care to join us for a meal to seal the bargain?'

James accepted gratefully, elated and excited. He hadn't expected to meet all his relatives quite so soon.

Polly MacDougal glanced round the dinner table with quiet satisfaction. She was presiding over one end and Joseph was at the other. She'd placed Evan Jones beside Lily, with James Cameron, the stranger, seated next to Rosie, where Polly could take a good look at him.

'Would you care for more vegetables, Mr Cameron?' she asked kindly.

'Thank you, ma'am,' he smiled, handing over his plate. 'It's an excellent pie. The best I ever tasted.'

Polly beamed. She'd already noted he was good-looking and had nice dark-brown eyes. His table-manners were good and he'd admired her cooking. Full marks so far, and yet . . . when he'd turned and smiled at her just now her heart had unaccountably missed a beat. He'd reminded her strongly of someone and it bothered her that she couldn't think who it was.

'Of course, I can guess what our Gracie's up to,' Rosie was saying, 'She's been chasing Sebastian Granton ever since she could toddle.'

'Aren't you just a little bit jealous, luv?' Lily teased. 'After all, Sebastian took you dancing once or twice.'

'Sebastian's not my type.' Rosie sniffed. 'I know some-body who's just wonderful on the dance floor.' Pity he's not wonderful in other ways, she thought, thinking of Edwin.

Polly frowned at her daughters in exasperation. Honestly, girls nowadays had no idea how to attract young men!

142

'Do you like dancing, Mr Cameron?' She turned encouragingly to James.

'Only Scottish reels, ma'am. I never learned ballroom dancing, I'm afraid.'

Polly gazed in desperation at Evan Jones, who could usually be relied upon to keep conversation going, but to her surprise, Evan was looking glum and she suddenly realized he hadn't said a word while everyone else was discussing Gracie's antics.

As for James Cameron, now he'd finished the meal he was sitting back in his chair, silently studying his hosts with what Polly felt uncomfortably was a critical eye.

It was a relief when Joseph began a long involved story about customers and cars. It did not interest Polly in the slightest but carried the diners safely through dessert and a cup of strong tea.

James had found meeting his new-found family more painful than he'd expected. As he'd watched his father sitting at the head of a table laden with good food, it had only served to remind him of his mother's desperate struggle to make ends meet over the years. He recalled the shame of his own difficult childhood compared to that of his half-sisters, born within respectable wedlock. How could he help but feel embittered as he watched this complacent little group? He only hoped it didn't show.

James glanced across the table to find Evan Jones watching him thoughtfully. As Joseph reached the end of a long anecdote, the Welshman gave James a faintly sympathetic smile then thanked their hosts warmly and stood up. 'If you'll excuse us, I must help James to settle in and show him the work we have in hand for tomorrow.'

James got up from the table gratefully.

Polly, smiling graciously, managed to hide her relief.

As Evan led the way through the garage, the racing car immediately caught James's eye.

'I say, that looks interesting! Mind if I take a look?'

Evan was delighted to show off the project so dear to his heart.

'Joseph designed the car and Sebastian and Grace helped him build it,' he explained eagerly. 'I work on it myself when I can spare the time. You see—' he unstrapped the bonnet to reveal the engine and went on more confidently – 'I hope to have this car in perfect racing condition when Gracie comes home. My dream is to drive it at Brooklands or Le Mans. Maybe win races. It – it is not for myself I want to win, you understand, it is just to please Gracie.' He glanced at James a little sheepishly.

For a fleeting moment James pitied him. Evan was the quiet, reliable type and in James's opinion, wouldn't stand a chance with Gracie against a handsome playboy like Sebastian Granton.

He turned his attention to 'MacDougal's Luck'.

The little car was certainly impressive. Many of his own favourite linkages and components had been used in its manufacture. But – 'I'm afraid this car will never be a winner at Brooklands or Le Mans,' he declared.

'Why not?' Evan demanded in dismay. 'It has loads of power!'

'Oh yes, the engineering's brilliant, but the chassis is too wind-resistant and the centre of gravity too high for cornering at very high speed.'

Now the faults had been pointed out to him, Evan was forced to agree that James might well have a valid point.

'So that's that. The end of a dream!' The Welshman sighed dejectedly.

'Not necessarily.' James was studying the engine intently. 'With modifications it could do very well racing on forest tracks. A Scottish motor rally, say—'

'It would be wonderful to win something for Gracie. Any race – anywhere at all!' Evan declared with sudden hope.

James was looking thoughtful.

'It would be better still if Joseph's car could race against Angus's new model – and win!'

'Yes!' Evan's eyes glowed at the prospect. 'Could it be done, James?'

'We could try, Evan—!'

The two young men stared at one another with shining eyes. Then James laughed and clapped Evan on the back.

'And may the best man win . . .'

Angus MacDougal's venture into the burgeoning motor car industry had caught the imagination of his entire workforce, and by the middle of March Sebastian and Gracie were well ahead with the construction of the vehicle.

'She's a beauty!' Sebastian enthused. All that was visible of him at the time was a pair of overall-clad legs sticking out from underneath the vehicle's running board.

Gracie laughed. 'Is that me you're admiring?'

'You too, of course, my love.'

She stopped work in sudden surprise. His banter was of the usual jokey kind, but the endearment was new. She glanced uncertainly at the legs, glad she didn't have to face him.

Love? Well of course, she'd always loved Sebastian, and she'd probably go on loving him forever. But Gracie's heart was filled to overflowing with various depths of loving. In fact, she loved nearly all the people she knew in some way or another.

'Hand me the pliers, will you?' Sebastian's hand came out from underneath the car, palm upwards.

Startled, Gracie realized that she'd never held his hand, not even to dance.

She knew he went to local Saturday night dances and was popular with local girls. He'd asked her to go dancing with him several times too, of course, but she'd always refused. Gracie knew that Mary-Jane felt responsible for her, and she didn't want to add to her landlady's worries now James had gone.

Gracie wondered what it would be like to hold Sebastian's hand, or to dance close to him. She wondered what it would feel like to be in love with him.

Hesitantly, she reached for the pliers and placed them gently in the waiting hand.

'Thanks, old girl!'

That was more like it! she thought, but the incident left her flustered and she was unable to concentrate on the job.

'I'm going outside for a breath of fresh air,' she announced.

Gracie felt better once she was outside in the pale March sunlight. A lane ran along the back of the works, and on the opposite side, a hedge marked the end of the MacDougals' garden ground. Through gaps in the hedge she could catch tantalizing glimpses of a glorious display of yellow, purple and white crocuses.

She stopped in wonder, then, with a quick glance round to make sure she wasn't observed, she wriggled through a gap in the hedge for a closer look.

The stolen view was worth it. The blaze of vivid colour was breathtaking in the sunlight.

'Beautiful, aren't they?' a soft voice said.

Gracie hadn't noticed the elderly lady standing quietly in the shadows, and jumped guiltily. She guessed at once who this lady must be.

She had learned from Mary-Jane that after her grandfather MacDougal had died years ago, her grandmother had seldom left the sanctuary of her own four walls. Janet MacDougal had only her son Angus for company.

'They're lovely, ma'am.' Gracie smiled shyly. 'I'm sorry, I know I've no right to come into your garden but I had to have a closer look.'

'Of course you did! Perfectly natural!' The old lady smiled warmly. She studied Gracie with interest. 'I haven't seen you before.'

'I'm a stranger here, ma'am,' Gracie replied, conscious of the irony. If only she could tell her grandmother who she really was!

'Oh, you won't know James Cameron then.' Janet MacDougal seemed disappointed. 'James used to come in for a cup of tea and a chat. He made me laugh, but he doesn't come any more. Angus says he's left the works. A pity.' She sighed and shook her head.

'Mother! You shouldn't be out without a jacket, you'll catch your death of cold!' Angus MacDougal came hurrying across the lawn but stopped short and scowled when he caught sight of Gracie.

'What are you doing here?' he demanded.

'Oh, don't be angry with her, dear,' his mother intervened. 'She only wanted to see the spring flowers.'

'Well, now you've admired our garden, you'd better go!' He glared ominously at Gracie.

She obeyed thankfully, heading for the gap in the hedge.

Her grandmother called after her, 'Be sure to come and visit before you go back home, my dear. Make me laugh!'

'Thank you. I'll try!' Gracie paused for a moment, smiling. How she longed to know this gentle lady better! But she heeded Angus's warning glare with a reluctant sigh and dodged through the hedge into the lane.

A dark cloud threatened to obscure the sun. Gracie shivered. That wretched family feud! Would it always cast a shadow over their lives?

Rosie MacDougal had found another job quite easily. Bertrand's Bakery had been established in Russian Road in the East End for fifty years or more, and was now in the experienced hands of young Bertrand, the grand-son.

Young Bertrand had jumped at Rosie after she'd spotted an advert in the shop window for an assistant.

'Smart young lady like you could attract a more classy customer.' He'd beamed. 'When can you start?'

On the strength of his approval Rosie had bought two white pinafores and two blue cotton caps off the barrows. She'd also scrubbed her fingernails and had another half inch snipped off a smart bobbed hairstyle before turning up at the bakery at seven thirty on Monday morning.

She sniffed the air appreciatively, enjoying the lovely aroma of freshly baked bread coming from the bake-house.

'What's that you're wearing?' Bertrand's jaw dropped when he saw her standing in readiness behind the counter.

'A pinafore, of course.'

'Why've you got an 'at on? Nothing infectious, I 'ope?' He eyed nervously a neat blue cotton cap covering Rosie's hair.

'Course not!' she frowned. 'Henry Heinz insists that his workers keep their hair covered when handling food.' She was annoyed to find herself quoting Edwin – she'd heard on the grapevine he'd secured a lease on a large corner shop and was spending money like water renovating and stocking the place.

'Well, you can tell Mr Heinz from me he'll never make a fortune in the East End, luv.' Bertrand stooped to pick up a loaf that had fallen off the board and tossed it nonchalantly back amongst the others. Rosie pounced and flung it in the bin.

'What you do that for?' Bertrand gaped at her.

'You can't sell that, it's dirty.'

'You'll learn, girl.' He shook his head ominously, 'You'll learn!'

And Rosie did learn in the course of a long, hard-working week. In fact, she had her eyes opened to a good deal of abject poverty. At the end of that first day she was distraught to find the dirty loaf had been quietly stolen from the bin.

When Edwin's new enterprise opened, Rosie couldn't resist the temptation to take a look. She stood well back on the opposite pavement when she reached Poulter Street, so that she was hidden by home-going crowds and busy traffic.

She had to admit the shop front was beautifully painted and the shop itself brightly lit. Inside, Rosie could see Grandma Hawkins sitting in a bower of flowers and Grandpa Hawkins looking splendid beside a cunningly-lit display of fruit and veg. Above the doorway was written in large gilded letters: 'HAWKINS EMPORIUM'.

Rosie stared wistfully at the shop she could never be part of. There was a lump in her throat that brought tears to her eyes.

'So what d'you think of it?' Edwin demanded cheerfully, appearing at her elbow.

'It's bright,' she said tartly. The wretched man missed nothing!

'Paintwork alone must've cost most of poor old Grandpa's life savings.'

'Rosie, Rosie! I never touched a penny!' He eyed her reprovingly. 'I hear you're working for Bertrand. You know . . .' Edwin looked thoughtful, 'we could do with a bakery supplier for our shop. I think I'll look in and have a word with Bertrand meself.'

Rosie tried to hide her horror. Bertrand's Bakery would never pass Edwin's stringent standards – at least, not in its present state.

'I'll tell Bertrand,' she promised weakly.

*   *   *

Lily MacDougal had made a determined effort to put the Reverend Matthew Peterson out of her thoughts. Yet every evening when she finished work her gaze would stray hopefully to the foot of the steps, where he'd once waited for her. He was never there. She was surprised how much that hurt. She'd loved and admired him for his devotion to the poor of his parish, yet he could go off to Africa and abandon all those who loved and needed him – and that included Lily herself, as well as all his poor parishioners in the East End.

The days were lengthening into spring, but the sun was low in the horizon on this particular evening, as Lily made her way wearily home after work. Its golden rays dazzled her as she stepped off the bus and headed for the archway leading to Granton Mews and she cannoned into a man standing in her path.

'Steady!' he laughed, catching her by the arms.

'You!' she said blankly, shading her eyes to take in dark clerical clothing, the white dog collar and Matthew Peterson's well-remembered smile.

Her one bleak thought after the first joyful leap of her heart was that at least he had come to say goodbye.

'Yes, me—' he said seriously, still holding her. 'After a great deal of soul-searching, Lily.'

'About going to Africa you mean?' she said sadly.

'Africa?' He shook his head. 'I'm not going to Africa. Not without you! No, Lily.' He linked her arm through his and they walked towards the arch. 'I've spent agonizing weeks wondering if it would be intolerably selfish of me to ask you to marry me.'

'Marry you?' she gasped weakly.

They had reached the shelter of the archway. She turned in the circle of his arm and looked up at him. It was shadowy and cool under the arch, but suddenly there was sunlight and warmth.

'My lovely Lily, I know I've no right to ask, but could you marry a poor preacher?'

'Of course I could,' Lily said simply. 'But – what about Marjory?'

'Marjory?' He raised his brows.

'Matthew, Marjory's so capable and kind! She would make a perfect parson's wife.' Lily was being despairingly honest. She knew she might be throwing her chance of happiness away, but this had to be faced.

He swept her into his arms and hugged her delightedly, laughing. 'Oh, my darling Lily! Marjory's a most worthy lady, but I don't happen to be in love with Marjory, I'm in love with you! I fell in love months ago with a girl I hadn't even seen, a girl with a smile in her voice and humility in her heart. A girl whose beauty and goodness will brighten the lives of those who live in Bright Street, if she'll agree to marry me—?'

'Yes, Matthew,' she whispered. 'Oh, yes!'

The sun was setting. Its fading light was soft and discreet beneath the archway as Lily slipped her slender arms around Matthew with a small sigh, and it felt rather like coming safely home after a long, uncertain journey.

So he is a man of God in clerical garb, dedicated to his church! she thought contentedly – but he is my man – my beloved – and I love him. Passers-by in the twilight who happened to glance curiously beneath the archway, might just make out two shadows merging, as Lily and her true love shared their first long, ecstatic kiss . . .

Gracie sat in a bus rattling homewards towards Kelso and chuckled delightedly as she read and re-read her mother's letter. Her sister Lily was to marry a clergyman and from the tone of the letter their mother was flabbergasted, delighted and absolutely bursting with pride. If Polly had

151

her way, the wedding planned later in the year would be the talk of the East End for months . . .

Gracie folded the letter with a smile and tucked it into her pocket. She stared happily out of the bus window at the town basking in hazy sunshine. Things were looking up. The new car was almost ready for the road, and she'd met her grandmother.

What's more, she'd decided that when Angus was safely out of the way at a business meeting tomorrow, she'd visit Grandmother MacDougal again. Uncle Angus had kept an eagle eye on Gracie since the incident in the garden, and she'd had no chance to slip away.

But tomorrow was the day!

The drifting haze had thickened as the bus approached her stop. Gracie frowned as realization dawned – it was not mist as she had thought at first, but drifting smoke.

She got off, anxiously alerted by sudden apprehension, and started to run. What she encountered as she rounded the corner stopped her in her tracks.

A small crowd had gathered outside Mary-Jane's house and she could see smoke pouring out of the wash-house at the rear.

Gracie ran on desperately, pushing past the on-lookers. At that moment Mary-Jane came racing round to the front door, smeared with soot and wild-eyed.

'What's happened, Mary-Jane?' Gracie grabbed her.

'I think one of the wash-house boilers exploded. There was steam and flames and smoke everywhere when I tried to get in – and I can't find the cat!' She clutched Gracie's hands, tears in her eyes. 'He must be in the house. Oh, Gracie, my poor Brimstone!'

Before anyone could stop her, Mary-Jane flung open the front door and darted inside. At once there was an ominous crackling roar as flames leaped up, feeding on a rush of fresh air.

'Mary-Jane, come back!' Gracie screamed.

Bella from next door appeared at a run, red faced and panting. 'Where's Mary-Jane? Tell her my hubby's got the cat and it's fine.'

The clang of the fire-engine's bell could be heard in the distance, but Gracie could not wait. She ran into the house after her employer. There was no sign of Mary-Jane in the sitting room, which was rapidly filling with smoke and unbearably hot, then Gracie heard her moving about upstairs, calling for the cat. She bounded up two at a time, dived into a bedroom and grabbed the older woman.

'It's all right! Brimstone's safe in Bella's house. He's fine.'

'Oh, thank heaven!' Mary-Jane looked as if she might faint. She sagged in Gracie's arms.

Struggling to the doorway, Gracie stopped in horror. Flames had reached the stairway, stairs and bannisters were crackling and burning and there was no hope of escaping that way. She retreated into the bedroom and slammed the door.

Mary-Jane was mumbling deliriously. The shock had been too much for her. Lost and bewildered, she muttered dazedly as Gracie half-carried her to the window and pushed up the sash.

Presently, a fireman appeared at the open window, brass helmet gleaming dully. With a struggle, she helped lift Mary-Jane out.

'Will you be all right, miss? Can you follow us down?'

'Yes, yes, just . . . hurry . . . with her,' she gasped. Smoke was curling in around the closed door, filling the room as he disappeared with Mary-Jane. Gracie was racked with coughing. Half-conscious, she sank down on the floor beneath the window, gasping for air, unable to move . . .

Polly was laughing. Her husband held one hand and she

had a small bottle of cider in the other. She felt very happy. Lily, bless her, was engaged to a clergyman and Rosie had a job in a well-established bakery. Clever Gracie was working with Sebastian Granton in Scotland and had healed a daft quarrel that had split Joseph's family for years.

Yes, Polly thought, life is good!

'I've never launched a battleship, let alone a motor car, so what do I do?' she laughed.

Polly, Joseph and the garage staff were congregated in the workshop round the finished car. A small naming ceremony was taking place before MacDougal's Luck began its trials. Polly was doing the honours.

'Don't hit my lovely car with the bottle, love,' Joseph said anxiously.

'Pour a little on the bonnet, Mrs MacDougal,' Evan smiled. 'Then we'll drink the rest.'

Polly obeyed solemnly.

'I name this car MacDougal's Luck. May it bring good fortune to all who travel in it.'

Joseph glanced round at the sound of a car in the forecourt, although it was evening and the garage was closed for the day.

'Can't they read the sign?' Joseph frowned in annoyance. He opened the door and looked out.

A young man was climbing stiffly out of his car.

'Sebastian! What are you doing here?' Joseph cried. A movement in the passenger seat alerted him. He beamed. 'Good lad! You've brought our Gracie home!'

'No.' Sebastian shook his head. 'I – I'm sorry. There was a serious fire in the laundry and Gracie has been taken to hospital. They say she'll be OK, so you mustn't worry,' he ended reassuringly.

The others had come out on to the garage forecourt. Polly gave a tearful wail at the news and Joseph put a comforting arm round his wife. James Cameron rushed forward, white as a sheet.

'My mother! What happened to my mother?'

'She wasn't hurt, James,' Sebastian turned to him sympathetically. 'But I'm afraid she's severely shocked. She keeps asking for you over and over. I couldn't find any relatives in Kelso and I didn't know what on earth to do for the best, so . . .'

He opened the passenger door and helped Mary-Jane Cameron out. She stood quite still, looking round with a vacant, puzzled expression. Then her gaze fastened on Joseph MacDougal and she paused – Mary-Jane studied the older man curiously, then gave a radiant smile of recognition. She held out her arms.

'Together again at last, Joseph my darling!'

Polly watched incredulously as the complete stranger approached her husband with outstretched arms.

'Joseph, who on earth is this woman?' Polly demanded loudly.

'Who on earth are *you*?' Mary-Jane glared at her.

'I'm Joseph's wife, o' course!' Polly retorted indignantly.

'W-wife?' A long exhausting journey had added to Mary-Jane's confused state. 'You – you can't be Joseph's wife!' she said uncertainly.

James Cameron hurried forward hastily and greeted his mother with a hug. 'You're muddled, Mother,' he muttered in her ear. 'This lady is Gracie's mother, Mrs Joseph MacDougal.'

'James! Have – have you told your father?' Mary-Jane was still flustered, but the sight of her son was helping to lift a cloud which seemed to have drifted over her mind.

'Shh! No, I haven't told him anything yet!' James said in an agonized whisper. 'How is Gracie?' he said loudly.

'I left her in hospital, poor girl! Oh, James, I thought

she'd died, I really did! She lay so white and still when they brought her out . . .' Mary-Jane began to sob. 'I feel so guilty. She saved my life and now she's suffering, while I don't have a scratch. It's my fault Gracie was hurt, you know, James. I ran into the house to find my cat and all the time he was safe with neighbours.'

'I'm sure Gracie will be out of hospital in no time, Mother.' James comforted her. 'And then she'll probably tell you how brave you were to attempt to rescue old Brimstone.'

The others had been hanging on every word. Polly was reduced to tears by now, and James sighed. To think the evening had started with a bit of harmless fun to launch Joseph's racing car! He'd never dreamed it would end like this.

'Would you mind if I took my mother to my flat?' He turned to Joseph. 'Perhaps she could stay with me till we decide what's to be done?'

'Good idea!' Joseph agreed thankfully. Mary-Jane would be out of Polly's way in the flat. The last thing he wanted was a confrontation between the two women.

Mary-Jane allowed her son to lead her away. Now that James had convinced her that Gracie would recover, she felt better. She smiled reassuringly at the others grouped anxiously around her. She still hadn't worked out who on earth they all were, but perhaps she'd sort that out later over a nice cup of tea . . .

Rosie and Lily had gone their separate ways that evening, leaving Polly and her husband on their own – which was just as well, Polly thought grimly, because she intended asking questions – and having them answered.

'Now, Joseph, who is that woman?' she demanded once they'd finished their meal and were settled by the fire.

'You mean James Cameron's mother?'

156

'Who else?' Polly gave him an exasperated glance. 'And don't tell me you never saw the woman before, Joseph, because I don't believe it.'

'She wasn't a washerwoman when I knew her, Polly.' He sighed. 'She was the daughter of the wealthy Cameron family and her station in life was a good bit above mine. MacDougal's in those days was just a country blacksmith's, though the business was growing fast.'

'So this fine lady fell in love with you!' Polly said dourly.

'Aye, we were in love.' He nodded.

All this had happened long before she and Joseph met, Polly knew, and hearing about Joseph's early love affair shouldn't hurt her. But it did!

'Well, I *thought* she loved me.' He frowned. 'We had even made secret plans to get married, but then – then – Polly, there was a death in my family.' Joseph paused, suddenly grief-stricken. The past came rushing back to torment him.

'Your father, Joe—?' Polly ventured. He'd always been reluctant to talk about his family, and tactfully she'd respected that and never pried.

'It was so unfair, Poll!' He looked wretched. 'My father cut me off without a shilling.'

'So Mary-Jane ditched you!' she cried indignantly. 'Did the fine lady take cold feet when your prospects suddenly vanished?'

'I suppose so. She left Kelso without a word to me and went to stay with an aunt in the far north. Soon afterwards the Grantons offered me the coachman's job and I left Scotland for ever.' He met his wife's eyes honestly. 'I swear to you I never heard from Mary-Jane Cameron again till she turned up here today. You're my true love, Polly.' He took her hand fondly and kissed it.

'Oh, Joe!' Tears welled up.

She was overcome with guilt. True? If he only knew the truth it would break his heart. She prayed he would never learn about her brief fling with William Granton, long over now.

She dried the tears, her thoughts returning to Mary-Jane.

'Why is she still called Cameron? She obviously has a grown-up son.'

'Maybe she reverted to the family name for business reasons. The Camerons had been successful in the town,' Joseph suggested.

'I bet she's divorced!' Polly pursed her lips. 'Nobody ever owns up to that! Her family would probably have nothing to do with her when the marriage broke up. She'd be forced to make ends meet washing clothes then.'

'You could be right,' Joseph agreed thoughtfully. 'I noticed James became very agitated when she mentioned his father.'

'Don't you worry, Joe dear.' Polly smiled and patted his hand. 'I'll have a chat with Mistress Mary-Jane Cameron when she's recovered her wits. I guarantee she'll talk to me, luv.'

Polly picked up some unfinished knitting and became engrossed in turning the heel of yet another sock, while Joseph lit another pipe to steady his nerves.

Nine

The hospital staff had assured Gracie she'd got off lightly and it was a miracle she hadn't been badly burned. All the same, she felt dreadful. Her throat was raw, her breathing painful and she ached all over.

But the real problem at this precise moment was anxiety. The nurse changing dressings on Gracie's minor injuries had just let slip unwelcome news.

Mary-Jane Cameron had left Kelso with Sebastian Granton, bound for London to join her son James.

Gracie groaned. If only Sebastian knew the trouble he'd caused!

'Is something sore, dear?' The nurse looked concerned.

'A – a headache.'

'Wait a tick, I'll bring you an aspirin.'

Aspirin would not cure this particular headache, but Gracie was too weak to protest.

She slept after swallowing the medicine and was dozing lightly when visiting hour arrived. She was roused by a man's voice.

'Gracie, are you awake?'

Sleepily, she opened her eyes and blinked in surprise at Angus MacDougal.

'How are you?'

'I should be discharged soon, with nowhere to go.' She stared at him bleakly. 'Then I'll return to London. I've nowhere else to go. You'll be rid of me at last, Mr

159

MacDougal. I bet you're delighted by the way things turned out.'

'Give me some credit!' Her uncle was outraged. 'I would never wish such a dreadful disaster on anyone.'

'You can't deny I'm an embarrassment though,' she persisted. 'So why have you come?'

'Your grandmother sent me. She insists that you come back to recuperate with us, at our house.'

Gracie sat up, wide awake.

'Does she know who I am?'

'Yes. After she read an account of the fire in the local paper I was forced to tell her the whole story. Now she demands to see you. Apparently my mother's been hoping for grandchildren for years.' He smiled faintly.

Gracie sank back against the pillows and studied her uncle. She'd worked for Angus for weeks, but felt she still did not know the man. And yet Mary-Jane had told her once that Angus was considered the most handsome of the three Macdougal brothers and was popular with the ladies in his younger day. She had even laughingly admitted flirting with Angus on several occasions at house-parties. 'He was so handsome and dashing and a really splendid dancer,' she'd added reminiscently.

Gracie frowned. She was sure she was overlooking something. It bothered her. Anything she could glean from his past might help her to understand this baffling uncle of hers.

'So shall I tell Mother you'll come?' he said.

'Oh, very well!' she sighed. She wanted to see her grandmother, but couldn't help wondering apprehensively what fresh problems she might be storing up for herself . . .

That evening, young Bertrand was wishing he'd never set

160

eyes on pretty Rosie MacDougal. If only he'd had the sense to put his foot down when she'd suggested cleaning up the bakery!

But she'd looked at him with that winsome smile . . .

'Of course!' he'd agreed light-heartedly. He'd get rid of that heap of weevily flour he'd been meaning to dump for months. Then he'd give the bake-house floor a quick whisk over with a broom . . . But not a bit of it!

Bertrand groaned. Rosie had insisted on a complete upheaval, so much so that his entire staff had worked late, scrubbing and limewashing the bakehouse. Families of mice and cockroaches that had existed happily undisturbed in store-rooms for generations, had fled the building. Most tiresome of all, Rosie had nagged Bertrand unmercifully until he'd shaved every morning and turned up to work in suit, shirt and tie instead of ancient fisherman's jersey and greasy dungarees. Then she'd produced white overalls and trilby hats for himself and staff. She'd ordered all that clobber from off the barrows – and expected Bertrand to pay for it.

When he'd raised strenuous objections she'd quoted the achievements of Sir Joseph Lyons of teashop fame. *His* waitresses wore spotless white caps and aprons and beaming smiles. Bertrand was forced to give in.

At last Rosie had declared herself satisfied with the bakehouse, and turned her attention to the outer shop. Fortunately only Rosie and Bertrand himself were involved in the planned assault.

He had already emptied the shelves of last week's bread, buns and scones which he'd piled in the side window on Rosie's instructions. These would be sold for a farthing the half-dozen, to the poorest.

'Aw, Rosie! The shop don't look too bad now,' Bertrand said hopefully, eyeing the empty shelves. 'Maybe we shouldn't bother.'

'You want to get ahead, don't you?' She glanced up with thinly veiled impatience. 'You want to make good?'

'Yes, but—' He was tempted to tell her that his grandpa, his pa, and he himself had made this business as good as it was likely to get, after three generations, and fifty years of hard graft in the East End, but she didn't give him the chance.

'Look here, Bertrand, you'd like to supply the best shops in town, wouldn't you? Remember when I told you Hawkins Emporium was considering Bertrand's as a supplier? I warned you that Mr Edwin Barlow, the – er – managing director, would inspect the bakery before placing an order.'

'Yes . . . we-ell . . .' he mumbled sheepishly.

'Mr Barlow said they'd go ahead with an order providing your place isn't too 'orrible.' Rosie's eyes flashed. 'The only problem is, Bertrand, the whole bloomin' bakery is an absolute disgrace!'

He should kick her out on the spot for darned cheek, but instead – he thought how vivid her blue eyes were when angry. They sparkled like diamonds.

'Yes, yes, I know, Rosie. I'm sorry, girl,' he muttered humbly. Ah, she was so pretty! He was like dough in her clean little hands . . . When she smiled, Bertrand wanted to bake dainty iced fairy cakes, tiny jam tarts and meringues light as summer's white cloud, to present to her on paper lace on a silver platter on bended knee . . .

Rosie had been in a state of panic ever since Edwin told her he would inspect Bertrand's premises. The trouble was, she had no idea when her step-cousin might turn up, though she'd no doubt he would choose the most inconvenient moment. The thought had driven poor Rosie into a frenzy.

Bertrand himself had presented the most serious challenge, but to Rosie's amazement he'd cleaned up quite presentably, if not handsomely. She was quite taken with him now that he shaved regularly, wore a clean white shirt and dark blue tie and had his hair neatly trimmed beneath the white trilby.

Poor Bertrand! Rosie smiled fondly at him as they surveyed the front shop. He was really very sweet and so eager to please. Most endearing of all, he didn't care tuppence what Mr Heinz did.

'You never know, Bertrand,' she smiled encouragingly, 'if we can maintain a high standard, one of these days we might be supplying Lyons' Corner 'Ouse. Maybe I should start serving our customers in black dress, frilly cap and apron. Now there's a lark!' she joked. 'Oh yes!' Bertrand sighed, drifting off into yet another delicious fantasy while Rosie, laughing, rolled up her sleeves and reached for the mop . . .

Angus MacDougal sent a taxi to collect Gracie from hospital. It smelled expensively of leather upholstery and was the largest car Gracie had ever sat in, but she wished her uncle had been sitting beside her. It would have been a friendly gesture to come to meet her, if nothing else.

The driver carried her case up the path and left her at the door.

'Good luck, miss!'

Alone and filled with trepidation, Gracie found the friendly remark ominous.

The doorbell was answered by an elderly servant struggling to conceal her excitement.

'Please come in, Miss MacDougal. You're expected.'

She took Grace's case and showed her into a large, airy sitting room. The windows were shaded by dark-green wooden venetian blinds, and sunshine slanted through, making bright sunlit patterns on carpet and furnishings.

The servant withdrew silently. Gracie's grandmother

had been sitting by the fireside, but rose when the door opened.

'How are you, Grace?' Janet MacDougal's welcome was not effusive. She held out a hand, which Gracie took after a moment's hesitation. 'Why didn't you tell me who you were when we met in the garden?' She sat down and motioned Gracie to sit opposite.

'I didn't think it was appropriate,' Gracie replied.

'But you said you were a stranger! That hurts.'

'But it's true, I *am* a stranger to you, ma'am.'

Her grandmother winced at the formality, but made no comment. Perhaps, like Gracie, she wanted to tread warily.

'Did your father ever mention me?' Janet MacDougal asked.

'No, ma'am. My father never mentioned his family.'

'No, I don't suppose he would.' She sighed.

'Look, ma'am, my father's a good man.' Gracie felt angry. 'I can't believe he'd do anything bad, yet you all treat him like a criminal!'

'Only to save him!' her grandmother retorted. 'Would you rather we'd pressed charges and made his crime public?'

Gracie stared, suddenly chilled.

'Crime? What crime?'

'You don't know?' Janet raised her brows. 'Well, I suppose Joseph wouldn't tell you. Embezzlement, theft. Call it what you like, my dear.'

'No! My dad wouldn't do that! My father wouldn't take a ha'penny that wasn't his!'

'Then poor Joseph has learned his lesson and taken it to heart. That's a great comfort to me!' Janet MacDougal smiled for the first time with genuine warmth. 'My dear, I'm sorry. I've given you a harsh welcome. Now let's start afresh.' She studied her granddaughter critically. 'Well, you're prettier than the MacDougal side o' the family, I must say. But so pale! Did the journey from hospital tire you?'

'I would have felt more welcome if my uncle had been there,' Grace admitted.

'Don't worry,' her grandmother laughed. 'Angus is more concerned about you than you might think. He stayed in the office today while the office girl went into town to arrange for some new clothes for you, since everything was ruined in the fire. Apparently you are about the same size.'

'Why yes, we are,' said Grace with surprise. She and the office girl had often compared notes during lunch break, and had discovered they shared similar tastes. Angus must have listened to their chatter, though he'd given no sign. Somehow this one small thoughtful gesture brought tears to her eyes.

'Time for Molly to bring in the tea-tray.' Janet MacDougal leaned across and gave the bell-pull a tug. 'Don't you agree, dear?'

'Oh, yes, Grandmother!' Gracie said gratefully.

A few days after Sebastian had arrived in London he appeared in Joseph's garage – as he usually did, sooner or later. It was an ideal opportunity for James to sound Sebastian out concerning the plan to enter MacDougal's Luck in a motor rally now the car was ready.

'A race?' Sebastian repeated thoughtfully.

'Yes. Between the two MacDougal cars – the English and Scottish. What d'you say?' James said.

'Rather! It would be wonderful advertising too, if either of them were to win a place.' Sebastian was immediately enthusiastic. 'Whereabouts exactly, Brooklands or Le Mans?'

'No. We need more difficult conditions than those. It's got to be somewhere that's a true test of car and

driver. We thought of a motor rally in the Scottish High-
lands.'

'It's a good job Angus MacDougal's car is built like a
tank.' Sebastian whistled.

'Yes, I know,' James said dourly. 'Don't forget I
designed it.'

'But we have modified and strengthened Joseph's car
too, look you!' Evan Jones chipped in. 'And it has the
speed!'

'Would it be against the rules for me to have a look?'
Sebastian gave the two a winning smile.

'I don't see why not, since you and Gracie practically
built the car.' James laughed.

The three young men eagerly unstrapped the bonnet
and were soon engrossed in a detailed discussion of the
engine's possibilities. Joseph MacDougal did not join the
discussion, though he was keeping a casual eye on them
through the open doorway of his office. He had intended
doing a little bookkeeping, but his thoughts kept straying
to the problem of Mary-Jane Cameron. He hadn't seen
her since her arrival a few days ago. James had insisted
his mother must have rest. Well, judging by the state of
Mary-Jane's hands and careworn look, there was no doubt
she'd been a hard-working woman! Joseph found it hard
to reconcile the middle-aged woman with the Mary-Jane
he'd known years ago, the pampered product of a wealthy
family. What had happened to change her circumstances
so drastically?

It was impossible to concentrate on the books that
afternoon. Joseph finally laid down his pen and left the
office, purposely avoiding the others grouped round the
car, and went out through the back door. Perhaps a breath
of fresh air would clear his head.

Warm sunshine and a stiff breeze had lured Mary-Jane
to the washing green behind the coach-house, which was

usually quite deserted. Today however, Joseph had chosen that leafy path to enjoy the fresh green leaves of spring.

They stared at one another in silent consternation when they met on the narrow path, only the width of the clothes basket between them and a host of memories springing awkwardly to life.

'How are you, Mary-Jane?' Joseph asked formally.

'Much better, thanks.' She lowered the basket slowly to the ground and looked at him.

In her right mind once more, after the trauma of the fire, Mary-Jane studied Joseph MacDougal. How could she have imagined he was the young man she'd loved? Time had moved on, and she saw before her an older man not in the best of health. Only the kindly, humorous expression seemed familiar, and the tender, sensitive mouth.

She shivered involuntarily, recalling how she'd had to stand on tiptoe to kiss him when they'd met in their secret hideaway deep amongst the hillside whins. How poignant the memories were! Did he feel the same?

'I'm sorry, Joseph,' she said humbly. 'I never intended to come back into your life. My wits deserted me, and Sebastian thought he was doing a good turn bringing me here to be with James. I plan to leave for Kelso now I'm fully recovered.'

'But your house burned down!'

'It can be rebuilt. The sooner I start, the better.'

'You're very brave,' Joseph said reluctantly, studying her. Why must he remember the indomitable spirit he'd cherished in the beloved younger woman? Why had she let him down so badly? It hadn't made sense to him then, and it did not make sense now.

An awkward silence fell between them.

'Well, at least some good came out of that wretched family feud, Joseph,' she said at last. 'I met Gracie. She's

167

a credit to you both, but . . .' She looked at him keenly. 'The family feud has given your poor daughter much grief. Why didn't you take steps to heal that dreadful quarrel?'

'How could I, since none of it was my fault?' His expression hardened. 'But of course you don't believe that, do you? You went away and left me in the lurch.'

'I had to go!'

'Of course you did. I was jobless, penniless and disgraced. Not much of a marriage prospect for you then, was I?' he mocked bitterly, his sense of betrayal as raw as if it had happened only yesterday.

'Stop it, Joseph! I can't bear it!' Mary-Jane cried brokenly. The English breeze was softer than the cool hill air she'd left behind, but her cheeks felt cold where tears ran down. She wiped them away, struggling to keep calm. 'I knew your brother, I knew what he was capable of. I never doubted for a moment you were the innocent one. You must believe me!'

He studied her in frowning silence. Some youthful beauty still lingered in the careworn face. He remembered suddenly that she had never lied to him, never denied him her loyal, generous love. His heart began hammering so that he could hardly breathe, and he put a hand to his chest. He could hardly bear to recall the sickening moment when he'd discovered she'd gone for good. There had been nothing for it but to shut his mind against the pain and get on with the rest of his life.

'Why did you go?' he asked, bewildered.

'Stop it, Joseph. It's all in the past.' She backed away, kicking over the basket of washing in her haste to escape.

'Oh no, you don't!' He seized her arm, pulling her close so that he could look down into her face. 'Mary-Jane, my dear,' he said more gently, noting distress in her dark-brown eyes, 'you *must* tell me why you changed

168

your mind and left me. You owe it to me – and to what might have been.'

She resisted strongly for a moment, then sagged in his grasp with a defeated little groan.

'If I'd stayed, I would have made it worse for you – your family, and mine, of course. I was expecting your baby, Joseph. Your son, James, was born in Thurso seven months after I left. But by the time I found out that you were living in London, you had married someone else.' She looked at him, sobbing quietly. The confession was hard, after all the years . . . 'I never told anyone who James's father was. James knows, of course, and that's why he came to you.'

'James – is my son?' Joseph's stunned gaze went involuntarily towards the garage where the young men were.

He had a son! An incredulous warmth spread through Joseph MacDougal's heart and mind. Someone to help him, someone to carry the business forward, the son he'd always wanted and needed in his life!

And then the next jarring thought was for his wife. Joseph felt weak at the knees at the very thought of Polly finding out.

Slowly, he let go of Mary-Jane's arm.

'What will you do, Joseph?' she asked anxiously.

'I don't know what to do for the best.' He shook his head. 'I've just found out I've a son who's a clever lad and an engineer like myself. I should be the happiest man alive, but – what will I tell Polly? She's already questioned me about you. She wanted to know why you called me darling.'

'I'm sorry about that. You see, for a moment I thought . . .' Mary-Jane hesitated, remembering that confused, awkward meeting.

'What did you think?' he prompted gently.

'That we were young again, Joseph.' She forced herself to meet his gaze honestly. 'But it was just a passing fancy. Polly soon made me see we'd grown older and love was dead.'

'Yes.' He reached for her hand and pressed it lightly. 'But friendship need never die, Mary-Jane.'

'Ah, but that depends on Polly, my dear.'

Just at that moment, James Cameron had left Sebastian and Evan deep in a technical discussion to stroll outside to look for Joseph.

He found him hand in hand with Mary-Jane.

James stopped abruptly, gazing incredulously at the scene before him. His mother and father together, an upturned clothes basket spilling clean washing on the grass beside them.

James strode towards them.

'What's happened?

'Joseph knows.' Mary-Jane turned to her son. 'I told him.'

'You – you did?'

This was a shock and James eyed his father warily. The two men had a good working relationship, but what did you say to a father you'd never known?

Joseph felt equally helpless. A warm hug seemed inappropriate and a friendly handshake could not even begin to express his feelings. Although he was not normally an emotional man, tears threatened as he studied his newfound son. Now his eyes had been opened, he must have been blind not to notice a resemblance to the MacDougals.

Of course, the young man had Mary-Jane's dark-brown eyes and thick dark hair, but James Cameron had inherited his father's height and cast of features. And his engineering skills, Joseph thought with a sudden lift of delighted pride. He laughed.

'James, I feel daft! I should have guessed you were my son. You're the only man I ever met that can change a tyre faster than I can!'

170

The small joke broke the ice. The next minute father and son were laughing and hugging one another, on the verge of tears.

At last, Joseph stood back, gazing at his son.

'I always wanted a son to follow in my footsteps, and now I have one! I adore my girls,' he added hastily, 'but – every man hopes for an heir to step into his shoes, I suppose.'

A reminder of his three half-sisters marred James's joy. There was bound to be trouble now.

'Who will tell Polly, though?' he asked anxiously.

'I will.' Joseph's smile faded abruptly. 'I'll choose the right moment and break it to her gently. In fact, it would be best to keep quiet about this till I've had a chance to speak to her, James.'

Mary-Jane watched the two of them together and sighed. She had a feeling there were many problems ahead, now her secret was out in the open. Quietly, she began gathering and sorting the scattered washing. It would be a sin indeed to waste such a fine drying breeze, she thought.

Gracie MacDougal wakened with a start in the strange bed, wondering where she was on the first morning in her grandmother's house. The mattress was soft and sumptuous after a hard hospital bed.

There was a gentle tap on the door and an elderly housemaid entered bearing a tray.

'Oh, my goodness, how kind!' Gracie sat up in bed. 'I didn't expect breakfast in bed.'

'Mistress says you're an invalid, Miss Grace. We have to spoil you.' She looked delighted at the prospect, tenderly arranging the tray across Gracie's knees and drawing the curtains to let sunlight flood in.

'What a wonderful breakfast!' Gracie smiled.

The maid lingered, eager to chat.

'Well you see, miss, it's grand to have a young person in the house. Jess an' me think it'll do the dear old lady good to have you to cheer her up.'

'Is she sad then?'

'Oh, she doesn't complain, but we've been with the family for years.' The maid sighed. 'Your grandma's had a long, lonely time of it since your grandpa died years ago. All this family feuding and fighting – daft, I calls it. Forgive and forget, sez I!'

Suddenly realizing she'd said too much, the elderly woman left hurriedly before Gracie could ask any more. But as Gracie tackled a boiled egg, she remembered something that had been niggling at the back of her mind. When they first met, Mary-Jane had let slip that she was at school with Joseph MacDougal's younger brother, then later on she'd again mentioned *three* brothers. Gracie paused with the eggspoon upraised. So there must be three MacDougal brothers! But where was the youngest?

The thought spurred her on to finish breakfast and dress quickly. She carried the breakfast tray downstairs and left it in the kitchen, then made her way to the front rooms, which were unoccupied at the moment. Her grandmother wasn't down yet and, of course, Angus would be long gone to the works.

Gracie welcomed a chance to search for evidence of the third brother. There were bound to be family photographs on display somewhere, she reasoned, if her own mother's crowded mantelpiece was anything to go by. Polly was intensely proud of her pretty daughters.

But after a thorough search downstairs, Gracie stood in the living room feeling completely bewildered. There was not one family photograph to be seen anywhere. Nothing – apart from an oil-painting above the fireplace showing a handsome middle-aged man Gracie correctly assumed to be Grandfather MacDougal.

How strange! Did Janet MacDougal take no pride in her three sons?

'You'll never guess where our Gracie is!' Polly said, glancing up from the letter she'd snatched up eagerly from the doormat just before they sat down to breakfast that morning.

Joseph, Rosie and Lily waited expectantly. Polly did not look delighted.

'Here was I, all ready to take the train to Scotland to bring her home from hospital, and now she informs us she's living in the lap o' luxury with her Grandmother MacDougal!'

'What's that?' Joseph's tone was sharp.

'Another grandma!' Rosie cried. She turned to her father with surprise. 'You've kept quiet about that one, Dad. I thought she was dead.'

'Can we invite her to the wedding?' Lily demanded eagerly.

Lily's heart, mind and thoughts were filled with nothing but her plans these days. She'd been warmly welcomed to her new family by Matthew's foster mother and house-keeper, Agatha Smithers. It was a hurdle Lily had been dreading, but Agatha had not compared any of Lily's shortcomings with the incomparable Marjory – in fact Agatha had seemed delighted when Lily had modestly admitted to imperfections.

'You an' me will get on just lovely, luvvie,' she'd beamed. 'Can't be doin' with perfection. Tires a body out, perfection does . . .'

'What d'you say, Joseph? Could we invite your mother?' Polly prompted. She eyed her husband speculatively. He hadn't said a word, sitting as if rooted to the chair.

'I doubt if she'd come,' he answered brusquely.

'Why ever not? She's Lily's grandma, after all!' Polly

snapped. 'Honestly, Joseph, I'm sick and tired of the MacDougals and their silly bloomin' squabbles.'

Polly was making up lists of wedding guests and was hard pressed to find family and friends she considered safe to invite to a vicar's wedding. According to Gracie's glowing description of the MacDougals' lifestyle, a few respectable Scottish relatives thrown in could lift the whole tone of the proceedings. If only Joseph could be persuaded to accept this proffered olive branch . . .

'I love squabbles,' Rosie said. She was in the midst of one with Edwin Barlow at the moment. She eyed her father. 'What's the MacDougals' squabble about, Dad?'

'You wouldn't want to know,' he answered grimly. 'I warned Gracie not to get involved, but she wouldn't listen, and see where it landed her. In hospital!'

'But recuperating in the lap of luxury – lucky thing!'

'Against my wishes!' Joseph frowned. 'I've a good mind to go and bring her home myself!'

'Well, why don't you?' Polly argued. 'Makes sense, Joe. You could thank your family for looking after her and give them an invitation to Lily's wedding. They'll be impressed to hear your daughter's marrying a clergyman. You can't get more respectable than that!'

'They'd shut the door in my face, Poll.' He frowned.

'Oh, I don't agree. A friendly gesture from you could put an end to bad feeling, luv.' She gave her husband an encouraging smile. 'It's worth trying, anyway.'

'You make it sound simple, Poll!' He sighed, shaking his head. 'It isn't so simple, though.'

'But you *will* go and bring Gracie home, won't you, luv?' she coaxed.

Joseph hesitated. He had left Scotland intending never to return, but he knew from past experience Polly wouldn't let the matter rest now. He would have to go and rescue Gracie – if only for the sake of peace.

* * *

James was in buoyant mood when Joseph appeared in the garage that morning.

'Have you told Polly yet?' he asked quietly, glancing hurriedly in Evan Jones's direction. The Welshman, fortunately, was out of earshot.

'I planned to do it last night, but she disappeared into Granton House with the girls all evening to sew dresses for Lily's wedding. She didn't come back till I'd given up and gone to sleep. Now Polly's persuaded me to go to Scotland and bring Gracie home. I can't break this shattering news to her, just as I'm going away. It wouldn't be fair, James.'

'Well, I daresay the secret will keep a little longer,' James said comfortingly. A thought occurred. Joseph's trip to Scotland might be used to everyone's advantage.

Eagerly, he told his father of the plan to race the two MacDougal models against one another.

'Would my brother agree to that?' Joseph looked doubtful.

'Sebastian's confident he would.'

'If so, Angus must believe he can win!'

'Ah, but the modifications made to MacDougal's Luck could easily beat him, especially if Evan is driving,' James declared confidently and went on, 'I happen to know there's an all-comers' motor rally in the Borders next week. I think we should enter the car and persuade Angus to do the same. What do you think?'

Joseph considered the scheme cautiously. He could see it had merits. In the excitement of a motor rally, with two young men to drive the car, his presence might go unnoticed. Once the race was over, he and Gracie could slip away.

'We'll give it a go,' he decided. 'Business is slack at the moment. Bert Smythe'll look after the garage if I ask him

175

to. He's a competent mechanic, and I know he hasn't had a regular job since he left the Army.'

Joseph smiled for the first time. Maybe this trip would not turn out so badly after all.

Evan Jones's eyes lit up when he was told of the decision.

'That is good news indeed!'

His spirits had been at a low ebb. He'd heard Sebastian Granton planned to return to Scotland soon, and was sure Sebastian meant to lay siege to Gracie MacDougal's affections, while he, Evan must remain in London nursing an aching and apprehensive heart.

He couldn't help envying Sebastian's undoubted charm with the ladies. He must seem a very ordinary chap to Gracie's eyes by comparison. All the same, Evan knew his own worth. He was tall and good looking and possibly one of the best mechanics ever to come out of the Welsh valleys. Girls liked him and gave him the eye, but he'd never fallen seriously in love till he set eyes upon Gracie MaDougal.

He knew he could be loyal, faithful and loving, but he had one glaringly obvious flaw – his limp. The broken leg, badly-set in prison camp, was the first thing people noticed. Once, he'd been a wonder on the dance floor. Light on his feet, with an unfailing sense of rhythm, other dancers had stopped to watch and admire. Now he would never dance lightheartedly with Gracie, never hold her close in his arms to the dreamy music of a waltz. He was condemned to limp crookedly for the rest of his days . . .

Forcing himself to concentrate upon the matter in hand, Evan smiled at the others.

'The race will be fine publicity for us if Joseph's car performs well. There must be a niche in the market for a fast sporty two-seater that will go anywhere.'

'Bound to be!' James agreed.

*   *   *

Everything fell neatly into place once the men began making final preparations for the trip.

Mary-Jane Cameron had decided to return to Kelso with Sebastian, who claimed he must make adjustments to Angus MacDougal's car before the race, as well as finalizing the sale of his parents' estate. She told James she would find lodgings with her friend Bella while making arrangements for the rebuilding of her house.

Evan and James decided to take turns driving Joseph's racing car to the Borders. That left Joseph occupying a seat in Sebastian's car along with Mary-Jane Cameron.

And how, he wondered, was he to explain that to Polly?

'Is something worrying you, Polly dear?' Lady Frances asked, studying Polly's troubled reflection in the mirror as the lady's maid fumbled with fixing her lady's hair.

'Oh, ma'am, I'm sorry! There's a hundred an' one things on me mind, what with Lily's wedding and all.'

'I'm sure the wedding will be wonderful. Remember the Armistice street party? You organized that, didn't you?'

'Oh, yes, ma'am!'

Polly wasn't likely to forget. That night she'd met William Granton in the mews to tell him their little fling was over. Joseph, absent so long in a German prisoner-of-war camp, was coming home. Gracie had overheard everything, and mother and daughter had been at odds ever since.

'So what's on your mind?' Lady Frances asked.

'Joseph. It's something serious. I can tell.'

'Oh, dear! Not his chest?'

'Oh, no, ma'am, thank goodness! Joseph's health has improved no end since James Cameron came to help him.

No, it's more like he has something on his conscience. He won't look me in the eye.'

'Ah!' Lady Frances breathed knowingly.

'He's going off to Scotland to bring our Gracie home, travelling in Master Sebastian's car with James Cameron's mother,' Polly explained. 'I don't like it, my lady.' She tightened her mouth. 'Joseph admitted he and that woman were more than friendly once upon a time. Suppose they're planning to run off together? He's been acting strange!'

'Then don't let it go on a moment longer, Polly! Do something. Now!' Lady Frances said urgently.

'But what, ma'am?'

'Confrontation, my dear! Confront him with your suspicions!'

Polly secured a wayward strand of her lady's hair firmly with a hairgrip and straightened her back.

'You're quite right, ma'am. I will!'

Ten

Rosie had arrived at work that morning to find a large basket of red roses on the bakery counter. Bertrand was standing beside it with a face like thunder.

'What's the meaning of this?' he demanded.

'I can't imagine. Me birthday's not till next Tuesday.'

She opened the little pink envelope attached to the basket and extracted the card.

> *To Rosie. On this special day,*
> *Love from Edwin Barlow XXX*

'Bloomin' cheek! He couldn't even get the date right!' she exclaimed indignantly.

'You can take your boyfriend's untimely offering out of my shop, Rosie, I don't allow flowers in the bakery,' Bertrand grunted huffily.

'Don't you worry. I'll put this lot in the store-room. Anyway, he's not my boyfriend.'

'Well, he thinks he is,' was Bertrand's gloomy rejoinder.

It was an extra busy morning, with a long queue of the poorest gathered hungrily outside the shop door. Word had got round that three trays of small meat pies had been dropped accidentally after baking and were to be given away on a first come, first serve basis.

Rosie was busy trying to control the pandemonium when

179

Edwin Barlow walked in to make a detailed inspection of Bertrand's Bakery, with a view to using him as a supplier for Hawkins' Emporium.

'You might've let us know!' Rosie wailed.

'I did. Didn't you get the flowers – and my note?'

'Yes, but I thought – oh, never mind!' Red-faced, she went on handing out pies.

'I'd be obliged if you'd kindly stop distracting Miss MacDougal when she's busy, Mr Barlow!' Bertrand boomed, appearing from the bakehouse. He made an imposing figure standing in the doorway, resplendent in immaculate whites. Rosie felt like cheering her knight in shining overalls.

'You heard the boss, Edwin. Remove yourself,' she grinned, popping a pie into a paper bag and twirling the corners. 'You may inspect the front shop later, when Mr Bertrand's introductory free pie offer ends.'

Beside the ovens, the two young men took stock of one another. Edwin was a sharp dresser, Bertrand noted. Dark pin-strip suit, maroon tie and white shirt with celluloid collar . . . Bertrand was glad he'd shaved extra carefully that morning and had donned clean overalls and dusted flour off the white trilby. Rosie was quite right, bless her 'eart! Clean clothes did give a bloke confidence.

'Where d'you want to start?' he asked.

'In the back alley,' Edwin replied grimly.

'OK,' Bertrand said blithely.

You could eat your breakfast off the flagstones in the back alley – Rosie had seen to that.

'The storeroom next, please,' Edwin ordered after he'd viewed the alley in silence, lifted the lids of sparkling, lined dustbins and poked around hopefully in clean, dustless corners.

Bertrand led the way and flung open the storeroom door. There was nothing to be seen in the tidy whitewashed area except a basket of red roses.

'My flowers!' Edwin gasped indignantly.

'Oh, I don't permit flowers on the premises on account of they attract flies, Mr Barlow. Rosie flung 'em in here the minute they arrived.' It was, Bertrand thought, a most satisfying moment.

There were already furious arguments between Polly and her daughter Lily over this wedding.

Lily favoured being married in St Martin's-by-the-Marsh, because she simply adored Matthew and loved every broken rafter and tumbled stone of his ruined charge. Polly, however, was quite determined the ceremony should take place in the beautiful Granton church – St Bartholemew's-in-the-Park. She dreamed of an elegant congregation packing the carved pews to watch her lovely daughter wed a clergyman.

In Polly's dream, Lily was a breathtaking vision in a flowing white satin gown, complete with long train and a perfect froth of lacy tulle veiling. It would of course be set off by a massive bouquet of orange blossom, lilies and perhaps a hint of white heather for luck – and in honour of the wealthy Scottish MacDougals – if they came.

But Lily refused to co-operate.

Lily fancied something very simple in cream silk, with a wavy calf-length hem and no waist. She intended, she said, to have a coronet of fresh flowers with a fingertip veil, and carry a small posy of tiny rosebuds made up by her darling Grandma Hawkins. Bright red, of course! Polly thought in near despair, her beloved Ma being an incurable romantic.

Wisely, Polly had decided she might lose the battle of the wedding gown, but she'd jolly well dig in her heels about the church.

'But Matthew's parishioners won't feel comfortable in our church, Mum,' Lily argued, thinking about old Archie

Winterbotham, who would not be parted from Julius, his beloved, faithful and unhygienic old spaniel.

Matthew Peterson was sitting in Polly's living room listening to the discussion. He hadn't taken any part in the argument so far, drinking tea and eating slices of Polly's excellent sponge cake, while pondering over the conversation.

Polly gave him a quick glance at this point. Matthew's presence made a frank expression of her opinion tricky.

'Your mother's right, you know, my darling.' He smiled at Lily. 'It *is* customary for the bride to be married in a church her family attends.'

'That settles it then!' Polly beamed delightedly. 'It's a lovely church for a wedding, Matthew. You'll be charmed when you look inside.'

'I'll be envious, ma'am.' He laughed. 'Lily tells me the organ works, the pews are padded and the steeple is still intact.'

'Er – yes.' Polly realized she'd narrowly avoided a complete disaster. She turned to her daughter. 'What bothers me is where to hold the reception, luv. There'll be a large crowd, and they'll be expecting to have a bit of a do, after the ceremony.'

'Why not hold the reception in St Martin's church hall?' Matthew suggested. 'It's large enough to house a battalion and my foster mother Agatha would be only too pleased to give you a hand with the catering, I'm sure.'

Polly wasn't familiar with Bright Street, but the name sounded admirably suited to a happy occasion and an ecclesiastical venue for the reception would look good on wedding invitations. Besides, it would please Matthew and his congregation.

'That would be wonderful, thanks!' she smiled.

She was so happy to have another thorny problem solved

she would have hugged the man – if he hadn't been a clergyman.

The moment the young couple were out the door, Polly headed for the garage to tell Joseph that two problems had been solved at a stroke. She came to a sudden halt as she reached the bottom step. Her husband and Mary-Jane were standing on the coach-house drying green, sheets flapping round their ears and so engrossed in conversation they hadn't noticed her arrival.

Mary-Jane saw Polly first, and her guilty start alerted Joseph, who swung round.

'Polly!'

She scarcely glanced at him, turning her attention instead to Mary-Jane and the sheets, curtains and table-cloths blowing in the wind.

'I see you intend to leave the coach-house the way you wish you'd found it, Mrs Cameron!' Polly sniffed.

'Once a washerwoman, always a washerwoman, Mrs MacDougal!' Mary-Jane replied cautiously. 'And by the by, it is *Miss* Cameron.'

She met Polly's eyes steadily.

'Mary-Jane, please . . . !' Joseph's whisper was agonized.

Polly turned to her husband in surprise and her heart almost failed her at his guilty expression. Was Joseph planning to leave her and go off with this shameless woman?

Polly almost wept. If he did go, she knew it was no more than she deserved. When she'd imagined herself in love with William Granton, Polly had been alone and lonely and hadn't known if her husband was alive or dead, but that was really no excuse . . .

Joseph's return from the war, faithful and loving as ever, had warmed Polly's heart and set her on the right path. Maybe not the dangerously exciting path she'd followed with William, but a pleasant way that renewed her self-respect and brought quiet happiness – until Miss Cameron arrived on her doorstep that is, and dark suspicions began.

'What's going on, Joe?' she cried tearfully. 'Whatever it is, I have to know, luv. Please tell me the truth!'

'Polly – I've been trying to, but you know how feeble I am with words.' He took her hand. It felt cold.

'Tell me. Please!' Her voice was barely a whisper.

Fear made Polly numb. She was convinced she was losing him – and now it was happening, she realized how much he meant to her. How could she go on, without her loving Joe?

'Very well, Polly.' Joseph squared his shoulders. 'You shall have the truth.'

Steadily, he told her the sequence of events right from the start, only glossing over accusations his family flung at him which were too painful to relate to anyone. When he came to the part where Mary-Jane left Kelso without a word, Polly came to life, incensed. She rounded on her rival.

'How could you leave him when he needed you? That was cowardly!'

'No, Polly.' Joseph answered for the silent Mary-Jane. 'On the contrary, it was very brave. I was in deep trouble enough, and Mary-Jane wanted to spare me more. You see – she had just realized she was expecting my baby.'

Polly tugged her hand from his and stepped back. Her cheeks had gone pale, her expression stormy.

'Your baby! And I thought you were a decent bloke!' she cried in disgust. 'Why didn't you marry her?'

'Because she didn't tell me, Polly, she just quietly made herself scarce. By the time the baby was born in the far north of Scotland, I'd met and married you in London. So Mary-Jane kept the secret to herself 'til Sebastian brought her to London. It was only then she told me I had a son.'

He watched realization dawn. Her expression changed.

'James! James Cameron is – your son?' Polly's voice shook.

Joseph nodded, unable to go on. When he did, the words tumbled out harshly.

'You asked for the truth. Well, now you have it.'

Dismayed, he watched his wife's eyes slowly fill with tears. He loved her so much, but there had been no kind way to tell her, no way to soften the blow. Polly knew him too well to be fobbed off with lies and half-truths. And he knew her anguish – could imagine the pain.

They gazed at each other silently, Mary-Jane forgotten for the moment. Both were thinking of the son they'd never had, the son he'd wanted so much. The son Polly had failed to give him.

Beloved, generous Polly! There was nothing he could do or say to help her now, but he had to try. Joseph stretched out a tentative hand and touched her arm.

'I'm so sorry, Polly. Can you ever—'

But she backed away as if she'd been stung, staring at him. Turning on her heel, she walked away without a word.

Joseph gazed helplessly after her. He felt close to tears as he watched his wife climb the stairs and go quietly into their flat. How he longed to comfort her, but what could he possibly say?

'Go after her, Joseph!'

'What?'

He started at the sound of Mary-Jane's voice. Momentarily, he'd forgotten all about her presence on the washing-green.

'What's the use?' His voice was anguished. 'You saw how upset she was. She'll never forgive me.'

'Rubbish!' Mary-Jane's brown eyes darkened. 'There's nothing to forgive! If Polly has to blame someone, let her blame me. I'm James's mother.'

'And I'm his father – who abandoned you both.'

'That was my fault. You didn't know.'

'Mary-Jane, no matter what you say, I can't forgive myself for getting you into trouble.'

'Listen to me!' She stepped off the grass and faced him. 'I'll never regret having James, because my son is the light of my life. But I will be heart-broken if his presence – and mine – should break up your marriage.' Mary-Jane smiled sadly and shook her head. 'Oh, I admit I despaired when my family threw me out and I found you'd married someone else, but now I can see it was the making of me, Joseph!'

She squared her shoulders and laughed.

'See? I became a tough wee Kelso woman who washed other people's dirty linen so's my clever boy could have an education. Did you know, I even schemed for James to become managing director of the family firm when Angus retires?'

'My son at the head of MacDougal's?' Joseph could see the irony. He smiled faintly.

'Aye.' She nodded. 'Till the famous MacDougal temper got the better of James and he fought with Angus.' She sighed and patted his arm. 'Ah, well, Joseph! Angus's loss is your gain. Now you have a fine son to help you get on.'

'That's all very well for me, but how will you manage?' He was concerned for her, all alone, growing old without her beloved son.

'Don't worry, I'll survive.' She shrugged. 'As for you, my dear, you're Polly's husband and the father of her three bonnie daughters. Why not go and convince her she's a lucky woman?'

'You don't know Polly!' He groaned. 'Can you imagine how she feels now she knows the son we both longed for isn't hers? What can I possibly say to comfort her?'

186

'Try a hug. Actions speak louder, as they say.'

'But . . . but what if . . . ?'

'Joseph Macdougal, will you kindly stop dithering and get going?' the little woman ordered.

He blinked, then turned and set off quickly down the path to the house, taking the stairs two at a time.

Joseph found Polly standing in the living room with her head bowed and her back to him.

He halted in the doorway. Was she still crying? He couldn't remember when he'd last seen his wife cry.

'Polly? Dear?' he ventured.

She turned, and he saw to his surprise that though there were traces of tears, she was quite calm.

'Quite an upset this is!' she said matter-of-factly. 'I was in a regular tizzy when you told me, Joe. I don't mind telling you I came rushing in here and shed a few tears. And then I looked at this.' He noticed that she was holding a framed photograph, the one of herself cuddling Gracie as a tiny baby resplendent in the Hawkinses' christening gown. 'Do you remember that day, Joe?' She smiled.

'Our Gracie's christening? Could I ever forget it!'

Standing shoulder to shoulder as they studied the well-loved photograph, the sweet scent of April Violets reached Joseph's nostrils, his wife's favourite perfume. His heart turned over. What on earth would he do if he lost her now? But she was still smiling.

'Do you remember how Gracie wriggled and the vicar nearly dropped her in the font?'

'Oh, yes!' He chuckled. 'She was only a tiny baby, but she nearly brought the roof down. Then Lily and Rosie started bawling in the front pew and you'd have thought the vicar was drowning the wee soul. It was bedlam!'

'Till Grandma Hawkins popped sweeties in their mouths!' Polly laughed. 'Then there was complete silence. Even our Gracie stopped yelling and behaved like an angel.'

187

'Aye.' He nodded. 'The wee darling was good as gold – even when fifty East Enders turned up for the christening party afterwards.'

'Joe, there were only fifteen!'

'Is that right, Poll? I could've sworn it was fifty!' Grinning, he dared to slip an arm round her waist. She didn't object. 'I always loved that photo of you both, Polly my darling.'

'Joe . . .' She hesitated a moment. 'Do you remember I cried for days after Gracie was born 'cause I'd set me heart on a boy and the doctor said there'd be no more babies for us?'

'Aye. I told you then that all that mattered to me was that you recovered your strength and our girls grew up to be healthy and bonnie.'

'And I wouldn't believe you!'

'Sweetheart, it was the solemn truth!'

'I know.' She touched the photograph tenderly with a fingertip. 'How proud I was of my baby daughter that day! Everyone stood around admiring the beautiful baby while Great-uncle Ollie fussed with that blessed plate-camera. He took ages to get everything set up, so I sat cuddling Gracie and watching you, Joe.'

She turned in the circle of his arms and gazed at him.

'You looked so happy! You sat with little Lily perched on your knee and an arm around our Rosie, and I suddenly realized that though we weren't blessed with a boy, I still had my health, we loved one another and we loved our little girls. After that, I never grieved no more.'

'You should've told me, Poll,' he said huskily. 'You never said.'

'What? With fifteen East Enders standing there, ears flapping? Not bloomin' likely!'

They shared a laugh, and then she said quietly, 'Joe dear, I'm glad you have a son, even though the boy's not mine.'

'Ah. Polly, my love . . . !' He was overcome with immense gratitude. 'I . . . I don't know what to say . . .'

'Don't say anything, Joe. Just . . .' She reached up and kissed him.

He gathered his wife in his arms and the kiss lasted a fair long time.

'Polly?' he murmured at length.

'Hmm?'

'Can you forgive me, dear?'

'Forgive you? What for, luv?' She lifted her head and stared at him in surprise. 'I can't think of anything.'

In Scotland, Gracie MacDougal was still puzzling over the lack of photographs in her grandmother's house. Not one, anywhere! It was frustrating. She was no nearer to finding out where the third MacDougal brother was.

When her grandmother came downstairs later that morning, Gracie hesitated to ask outright. It was obviously a delicate subject and she was afraid it would upset the old lady.

'Well, Grace, you're looking much better this morning!' her grandmother remarked, smiling.

'I feel better, Grandmother. Breakfast in bed was a treat.'

'Oh, Jessie's invalid breakfasts are always appreciated, my dear. It's almost worthwhile being ill, I say!'

She settled herself in the drawing-room and smiled at her granddaughter.

'So what will you do with yourself this morning, Grace? How about exploring the garden and round about? Fresh air will do you good.'

'Won't you come with me?'

'Bless you, no!' Her grandmother laughed. 'I couldn't keep up with you. I just dawdle along. No, Grace, I shall open the mail and read the papers till your Uncle

189

Angus comes for lunch at twelve thirty.' She fitted on her spectacles and picked up a newspaper. 'You'll hear the dinner gong quite clearly out in the grounds, so be sure not to miss lunch. It's Jessie's speciality today – lamb chops, garden peas and Ayrshire potatoes.'

Gracie went outside into a glorious sunny morning. Smiling, she lifted her face to a brisk breeze which Mary-Jane would have made good use of. How, Gracie wondered, was Mary-Jane getting on in London? There had been no frantic letters from James or her parents on that score, so she decided no news must mean good news.

The front garden was well tended but dull, so Gracie made her way to the rear of the big house through a walled garden well stocked with fruit and vegetables. Leaving the garden, she discovered a wooded area that was much more to her liking. Trees and flowering shrubs grew in profusion and an intriguing woodland path wound enticingly into leafy shadows.

Gracie followed it eagerly, her footsteps hollow on a path laced with tree roots. It was all such a far cry from London streets, she was almost disappointed when the woodland grew sparse and she found herself on the bank of a fast-flowing river.

This was not the broad River Tweed itself, she realized, but quite a sizeable tributary. White water tumbled over rocks from the hillside beyond, which was ablaze with yellow broom. The falls spilled into a black pool fringed with reeds.

An elderly fisherman stood on a footbridge. As Gracie watched, he cast a line, then raised a hand in salute.

Encouraged, Gracie approached on tiptoe.

'Any luck?'

'Not a nibble. Sun's too bright, miss.'

He had a weatherbeaten, whiskery face, with keen blue

190

eyes that disappeared with a twinkling gleam into a criss-cross of wrinkles. 'Och, I warned Jessie there'd be no trout for the table tonight, but would the woman listen to the voice o' experience?'

'Are you from the house then?'

'The gardener's cottage, miss. I'm Sam Wylie, the handyman. I've worked for the MacDougals for years. My father was a wheelwright when they were just country smiths.' He eased the line gently to follow a ripple down the pool, then glanced at her. 'I ken who you are, though. Jessie told me Master Joseph's lassie was staying.'

'That's me! Did you know my father, Mr Wylie?'

'I knew all the MacDougal sons from when they was wee laddies.'

'You mean Angus, Joseph and – who was the other one?' She tried to appear casual though she held her breath, hanging on the answer.

'Patrick the youngest? Oh, aye, I knew him!' Delicately, he reeled in slack so that the bait hovered in the eddy.

'Where is Patrick now?'

'You don't know?' He gazed at her in surprise. 'Aye well, I don't suppose your dad would tell you. He shouldered the blame.'

'Blame? What for?'

'Och, lassie, for everything of course!'

At that point the tip of the rod dipped and the line tightened. The fisherman cheered.

'A bite at last! A big 'un, by the feel of it! Trout for yer supper after all, missie!' he chortled.

Frustrated, Gracie left him to do battle with a lively catch. She could see she'd get no more information meantime.

The muffled tones of the dinner gong rang out across the woodland. Gracie broke into a run, retracing her steps, but her uncle and grandmother were seated at the table by the time she'd washed her hands and tidied her hair. She took her place apologetically.

'I must say you're looking much better today, Grace.' Angus studied her kindly.

'Of course she's better!' his mother said crossly. 'My granddaughter needs fresh air and good food at the moment, Angus,' the old lady went on querulously. 'I can't think why Joseph is coming to take the poor girl back to that filthy city!'

'My dad's coming here?' Gracie cried incredulously.

'He's on his way,' Angus said nodding. 'A letter arrived in the office this morning.' He reached into his pocket and produced it. 'And apart from escorting you home, Grace, the purpose of your father's visit is to challenge me to a race.'

'What sort of race?' she asked, intrigued.

'A motor rally. There's one in Glentarn forest at the weekend. Your father wants to enter his car against mine in the standard class cross-country event.'

'You didn't tell me about this!' His mother looked dismayed.

'I was going to, Mother. Don't worry—' he glanced at her kindly – 'you don't have to meet Joseph.'

'You think that worries me?' She sounded annoyed. 'I'm worried because motor racing's a dangerous game. Someone's bound to get hurt—'

'And then I suppose my father will get the blame!' Gracie said.

They turned and stared at her.

'What do you mean?' Angus demanded sharply.

'Nothing. I – I'm sorry.'

Fortunately, the door opened at that moment and in came Molly the housemaid bearing a tray containing a sizzling platter of lamb chops surrounded by dishes of fresh vegetables.

The old lady turned with relief to the elderly servant. A brass clock on the mantelshelf chimed the half hour.

'Ah, Molly dear, on the dot, as usual!'

'I shan't go to the office this afternoon,' Angus decided when lunch was over. To Gracie's relief there had been no more talk of motor rallies. He smiled at her. 'I thought we might take Grace for a spin in the Morris this afternoon, Mother.'

'Good idea, Angus dear, but forgive me if I don't join you,' his mother said. 'I shall read my book in the summerhouse, then take a stroll in the garden later, when it's cooler.'

Gracie was delighted to fall in with her uncle's suggestion. Angus lowered the Morris's canvas hood to take advantage of the fine weather and provided Gracie with goggles and a chiffon scarf to keep her hair tidy.

He seemed more approachable as he drove along country roads pointing out places of interest, and Gracie plucked up courage to speak.

'I talked to Sam Wylie this morning,' she began.

'Oh, yes?' He immediately sounded wary.

'He told me he knew all three MacDougal brothers, yourself, my father – and Patrick.'

He didn't speak for a moment or two. Frowning, he changed down to negotiate a sharp bend.

'What else did old Sam tell you?'

'Nothing much. He was too busy catching trout. So where is my uncle Patrick?' she demanded. 'There are no photographs of any of you in the house. Not one photograph, anywhere. I find that very strange.'

'You're an astute young lady, Grace MacDougal!' He glanced at her with a hint of admiration.

'I'm not a true MacDougal, Uncle. I hate secrets and I never bear grudges.'

'Ouch!' He winced with wry humour.

'So where is Uncle Patrick? And why are there no photographs?'

'Have patience, Grace.' He sighed. 'I'll show you.'

He made a sharp left turn off the road at the next exit. The minor road narrowed after two or three miles and they came to a cluster of houses built on the edge of fields.

A loop of the river meandered past a farmland village and the road crossed a bridge which cast dark shadowy reflections on the water beneath. A small church stood close by, its graceful spire pointing to the sky.

Angus pulled up outside and helped Gracie out.

'This is where the MacDougals worship. Come inside.'

Gracie followed her uncle into the church's cool interior. There was nobody about, no sound save their footsteps echoing in the high arches of the nave. The walls were panelled in dark wood but light streamed in through a large stained-glass window in the eastern wall, making the empty silence less oppressive.

Angus had gone ahead and was standing by the tall window.

'Here, Grace!'

She crossed over and stood quietly beside him.

This window was quite unlike any she'd seen in churches, depicting biblical subjects.

Instead it was a perfect replica in coloured glass of a footbridge, a river in placid mood with trees, golden broom and a green hillside beyond. In fact, it was remarkably similar to the scene she'd viewed that morning when she'd met old Sam Wylie.

Studying details of the beautiful window more closely, she saw there was a single bird flying heavenwards in the azure sky, a dark, swift bird on scimitar wings flying fast and free into a glory of sunlight that bathed the church in golden light. Soft grey clouds massed close to earth somehow imparted an unbearable sense of loss and pain.

Gracie read the inscription beneath.

Sacred to the memory of Patrick Henderson MacDougal, aged 19 years.

Bemused, she turned to her uncle.

'Patrick . . . ?'

'My youngest brother.' He nodded gravely. 'Patrick drowned.'

Suddenly she saw the horror of it all.

'And you blamed my dad!'

'Yes.' Angus MacDougal looked acutely uncomfortable. 'They were heard arguing fiercely down by the river. I was hurrying to separate them when I heard Patrick threatening to tell Father what Joseph had been up to – we discovered later that Patrick had checked Joseph's accounts and found serious discrepancies in the ledger. Then I heard a terrific splash and when I arrived on the riverbank, Patrick was struggling in the water. Before we could reach him he was swept under the bridge and disappeared.' He paused for a moment, reliving the awful moment. 'My mother never got over the tragedy, Grace. Patrick was the apple of her eye,' he said sadly.

Gracie gazed at the beautiful window. Tears welled up and spilled down her cheeks.

'I can't believe my dad would do something like that.'

'He swore to us that the bank was slippery and Patrick lost his footing.' Angus sighed and shook his head. 'Well, maybe so, but my brother would be alive today if Joseph hadn't been thieving. I'm sorry, Grace, but now you will understand why we can never forgive your father.'

Eleven

The peace and quiet at breakfast the morning after the menfolk left for Kelso gave Polly an opportunity to tell Rosie and Lily that James Cameron was their half-brother.

There was stunned silence.

'What – what will you do, Mum?' Rosie asked finally.

'What d'you expect me to do?'

'You won't accept him into our family, will you?'

'Why not? Your dad always wanted a son. I'm delighted for him.'

'So his daughters were a disappointment, were we?' Rosie said in hurt tones.

'Of course not!'

'You can't kid us, Mum!' Rosie wailed. 'James Cameron will be his favourite. Come on, Lil!' She rose abruptly from the table. 'Let's go to work. I couldn't swallow another bite!'

Lily stood up, on the verge of tears. What would Matthew say when he heard about this shocking state of affairs? He was a clergyman, after all!

The two sisters left the kitchen and Polly winced as the outer door slammed.

It was unfortunate for young Bertrand that Rosie arrived in a bad mood that morning. He'd had good news yesterday.

196

'We got the order for Hawkins Emporium, Rosie!' he announced.

'So what's an emporium?' She eyed him moodily.

'It's sort of . . . it's kind of . . . um . . .' He was stumped.

'You don't know either,' she said accusingly.

'Well, no wonder!' he declared, stung. 'Trust high-and-mighty Mr Edwin Barlow to come up with something nobody never heard of. Why don't your Edwin call it a shop like other traders?'

' 'Cause Edwin Barlow doesn't think like other traders!' she retorted. 'And he's not my Edwin.'

'Isn't he?' Bertrand's good humour was restored. He had a vision of pale pink and white iced cakes topped with red sugar roses, nestling on a lacy paper doily and hidden under the counter. He'd made them specially for her and would present them, once he'd said his piece . . .

Angus MacDougal felt sorry for his young niece. Her father's part in the family tragedy had obviously depressed and upset her. He had decided that a trip to the works to cast an eye over the finished car she and Sebastian had helped to construct would be the very thing to cheer her up.

Gracie was finding the visit a rewarding experience. The finished vehicle looked very impressive, and –

'You've made it British racing green!' Gracie exclaimed delightedly.

'Did you have racing in mind, Uncle Angus?'

'No, I didn't. I just wanted anything but black.' He smiled, then became serious. 'This car's designed for touring, you see. Any chance of success it will have in the rally depends upon Sebastian's driving skill and my knowledge of the course. And the four-wheel drive James Cameron designed, of course.'

'Would you take James back if you had the chance?'

'Yes, I would.' He didn't hesitate. 'The lad's quite brilliant.'

'Better than me, Mr MacDougal?' There was a chuckle behind them. Gracie whirled round delightedly. 'Sebastian!'

He returned her hug, reluctant to let go, then kissed her warmly. Gracie blushed hotly and hastily disentangled herself. She had noticed Evan Jones standing in the doorway, watching this public display of affection. Sebastian casually waved a hand in Evan's direction.

'By the way, Mr MacDougal, this is Evan Jones. He'll be driving your brother's car. Would you mind if he has a look at the opposition?'

'Oh, very well, Sebastian,' Angus agreed somewhat reluctantly.

Evan came forward and paused in front of Gracie.

'It does my heart good to find you well.' He took her hand. 'I think it was the blackest day of my life when I heard you were in hospital.'

'Thanks, Evan,' she said, warmed by his sincerity. She watched him limp across to examine the rival vehicle, then she turned eagerly to Sebastian. 'Has my dad arrived?'

'Yes – and he's longing to see you! But he won't come here.' He cast a meaningful glance in Angus's direction. 'He and Evan have taken lodgings in Kelso.'

Angus MacDougal had been studying Evan shrewdly while he examined the engine. This lad knew what he was about all right! He'd be a serious contender. Still, he'd need a first-class navigator – on six miles of treacherous woodland track it was all too easy to take a wrong turning and lose valuable time.

'I suppose James Cameron will be your navigator?' he asked.

'No, sir.' Evan looked up. 'James will be needed at control points to take care of repairs. Joseph MacDougal

198

will navigate for me. He knew the forest well at one time, he says.'

And I'm to be Sebastian's guide! Angus thought grimly. Brother versus brother. What an intriguing prospect.

Janet MacDougal had dug her heels in over this rally.

'If you think I'm going to sit at home worrying myself sick about you all, you're sadly mistaken, Angus!' the old lady told him.

'Very well, Mother.' He sighed. 'I'll ask Sam Wylie to drive you and Grace to watch proceedings in the Morris. Will that satisfy you?'

'I suppose it'll have to,' his mother groused.

The sky was dark with rainclouds when the morning of the rally dawned. Sam Wylie knew every twist and turn of obscure paths through the forest and drove his lady passengers to a sheltered vantage point.

Janet MacDougal insisted on getting out of the car to watch the Glentarn rally more closely.

'I must say the track looks perfectly dry and safe, Grace,' she remarked to her granddaughter, once they were seated, a tartan rug tucked around her elderly knees.

A horn sounded five cheeky blasts as a car appeared round the bend, travelling fast.

'Here they come! Is that ours, Grace? Are we winning?' Janet yelled, raising opera glasses.

'No, no, it's a Fiat, and there's an Austin close behind!' Gracie watched the two cars skid sideways round the bend, one after the other. 'We won't know the winner till the results appear on the leader board, you know, Grandmother.'

'Oh, I can hardly wait! Where are our boys?' The old lady stared anxiously along the course as more mud-spattered cars roared past.

Gracie was worried. The threatened rain had started quite

heavily and she could see the leading cars had churned mud at the bends into deep ruts. The track would soon be a quagmire.

At last two cars Grace recognized came hurtling round the corner. 'Evan and my dad are in front, Sebastian and Uncle Angus are just behind!' she yelled excitedly.

'Joseph!' Janet whispered. She put a hand to her mouth.

Gracie never knew whether Evan and her father had spotted them at that crucial moment and lost concentration for a vital second, but suddenly the small car lurched into a deep rut, skidded off the track and came to rest, its wheels spinning in slippery mud.

Sebastian's two-tone horn honked derision at his struggling rivals. Angus MacDougal kept his head down, concentrating on the pace notes which kept track of their progress, but Sebastian blew Gracie a kiss as he went storming past.

'Winner takes all, my darling! Winner takes all . . . !'

The car sped on and she stood staring after it. So this had become more than just a race, it was a contest, between two young men who were suddenly deadly rivals.

Her father had leaped out of the stranded vehicle and was pushing and shoving and struggling for breath. Gracie came to life.

'Come on, Sam, let's lend a hand!' she shouted to their driver, who was standing by the Morris. The old man obeyed with alacrity.

'Here, Grace! You'll need this!' Her grandmother tossed the tartan rug across to her.

Joseph and Sam shoved manfully, but it was the rug that saved the day. Gracie spread it over the mud to give the front wheels purchase, Evan coaxed the engine gently and the car slowly pulled out of the clinging ooze on to firmer ground.

'Well done, Gracie!' Behind mud-spattered driving goggles Evan's blue eyes shone bright and clear.

Her father vaulted into the moving car. Janet MacDougal
had made her way hesitantly to the edge of the track and
for an instant mother and son faced one another.

Janet stared, shocked. She could see her son had aged and
suffered greatly, but he was looking at her with Gracie's
eyes. Clear blue, honest, utterly trustworthy.

Janet put a hand to her heart. Its sudden agitation made
her feel breathless. Had injustice been done all those sad
and terrible years ago?

'Good luck, Joseph my dear!' she heard herself cry out
strongly.

'Thanks, Mother!'

His smile was loving, but his mother could have wept.

Evan put his foot down and the car and its occupants
skidded round the next bend, throwing up a drenching
spray of mud.

Gracie wiped a muddy trickle off her chin.

'They've lost so much time they'll have their work cut
out to beat Sebastian and my uncle.'

Her grandmother dabbed at moist eyes with a muddy
hanky.

'Oh well, dear, I suppose it's just a race!'

But Gracie knew better. Men and cars were being
tested to the limit in bitterly fought rivalry. At the end
of the day would she be expected to choose between a
much-loved father and an uncle she'd grown to like and
respect?

Or for that matter, between two young men she loved
and admired? Gracie shivered, she imagined she could still
hear Sebastian's triumphant cry.

'Winner takes all, my darling! Winner takes all . . .'

'That'll be the last car in the present series.' Old Sam
Wylie had been keeping count. Now he consulted his watch

as three more cars skidded past the vantage point. 'Maybe we should tak' a look at the finish, ladies.'

It was a hazardous journey even allowing for Sam's extensive knowledge of forest tracks. Eventually they arrived in an open field just as the rain stopped and a watery sun broke through the clouds.

A wet but cheerful crowd had congregated round the finishing line. Time-keepers and officials occupied a large marquee nearby and an interested group of competitors was gathered round the leader board. Farther away, a line of parked cars caked with mud showed evidence of hard driving. Drivers and mechanics stood around in groups, talking motors.

'I don't see them, do you, Grandmother?' Gracie said anxiously.

'No, dear.' Her grandmother raised the opera glasses. 'But I can see a small car coming in all on its own. Could it be your father's?'

'Aye, it's your dad right enough, Miss Grace.' Sam Wylie frowned. 'But something's wrong. They're slowing down.'

'Oh, no!'

Gracie scrambled out of the car and headed for the stone dyke which ran alongside the track, clambering up it to gain a better view. Sure enough, her father's car was the only one in sight. Evan must have driven superbly to have gained such a lead, but the car was definitely much too slow.

She groaned as she saw another car come roaring round the last bend. How disappointing to be overtaken on the finishing line!

'Come on, Evan!' she yelled.

The car lurched and juddered as it came abreast, and she could see at once what the problem was. The tyres had punctured and the car was running on metal rims.

'Come on, Evan! Come on!' she cried frantically.

But it was too late. Her uncle's car thundered past, nearly knocking Gracie off her perch. Then came the triumphant blast of a horn and an exultant yell from Sebastian.

'We did it! We won!'

She didn't see Evan inching McDougal's Luck across the line seconds later. Her eyes were too blurred with tears.

Old Sam had fresh information when Gracie trailed disconsolately back to the Morris.

'They're saying the Talbot is overall winner, but Mr Angus won the contest between the two brothers, miss. That's created a fair bit o' interest here today, I'm tellin' ye!'

'Tyres let my father down,' Gracie sighed.

'Aye. Tyres'll do that.' He nodded sympathetically.

Janet MacDougal watched her granddaughter. The poor girl couldn't hide her deep disappointment.

'Why don't you go and speak to your father, my dear?' she suggested kindly, then added hesitantly, 'And – and maybe you could ask him to come and speak to me—?'

'Yes.' Gracie smiled. There was a ray of hope to brighten the day, after all. 'I'll tell him that, Grandmother.'

Gracie was trying to worm her way through the large crowd when Sebastian appeared out of nowhere and grabbed her. Eyes shining with excitement, he lifted her off her feet and whirled her round.

'I won, Gracie. I won!'

'No. you didn't,' she said breathlessly. 'Sam says the Talbot did.'

'Oh, we hadn't a hope of winning the rally, Gracie!' He grinned. 'But I beat Evan Jones. That was the contest. And the winner always gets the girl, don't you know?'

He reached for her tenderly, but she put a hand on his chest before he could land the kiss.

'Not so fast! That contest was null and void. Evan would have won if it hadn't been for punctures.'

'You know what, Gracie MacDougal?' His expression darkened sulkily. 'Why can't you be a pretty little brainless flapper, and not a female engineer with a mind accurate to one thousandth of an inch?'

'Why thanks, Sebastian dear. What a wonderful compliment!'

She smiled impishly and dodged out of his grasp, to leave him spluttering behind her.

Evan Jones's heart had leaped when he spotted Gracie cheering. Then doubts set in as he'd struggled on with tyres shredding to pieces. Was she cheering for him – or Sebastian? The thought had hardly entered his head when Sebastian roared past them.

Evan's spirits were low as he parked the little racer in the field beside the others, but Joseph was cheerful.

He assured Evan they'd only been beaten by broken glass from the shattered headlamps of another car. He praised Evan for a magnificent drive and declared that if there was any justice in this world, they should have beaten his brother Angus.

Joseph went off quite jauntily to study the leader board, leaving the younger man scanning the crowd eagerly for Gracie. He had to see her if he was to have any peace of mind. He loved her and believed he could tell if there was any hope for him the moment he looked into her honest eyes. They never lied!

The crowd parted for a moment to let a car come through, and he had a clear view of Grace MacDougal clasped lovingly in Sebastian's arms. Evan stopped dead, too shocked to move. He watched his rival swing Gracie off her feet, her arms round his neck as they whirled joyfully. Then the car passed and the crowd closed in and hid the couple from sight.

Evan turned on his heel and limped furiously away, pushing his way past spectators, back to the car.

James was moodily picking remnants of burned rubber off the wheel rims. He looked up when Evan arrived with a face like thunder. Evan said nothing, just reached grimly into the driver's seat and gathered up his gear.

'What's up?' James frowned.

'I'm saving your father the embarrassment of giving me the sack. I'm leaving.' Evan stuffed driving goggles into a pocket and held out a hand. 'Goodbye, James, and good luck. We were a fine team.'

'What about Gracie?'

'What about her?'

'I thought—'

'So did I.' His eyes were cool and angry. 'Weren't we the fools?' He turned and limped across the grass. The buses stationed at the far end of the field were filling with chilled spectators heading home. Evan planned to be out of Kelso before Joseph could find him and persuade him to stay.

Joseph and Angus MacDougal had been hoping to avoid one another, but they met suddenly face to face beside the official marquee. There was an awkward silence between the brothers, then Angus spoke.

'I must say I admire your sporty little car, Joseph. It should appeal enormously to younger drivers.'

'You think so?' The praise caught Joseph off guard. 'You deserved to win, Angus,' he said sincerely. 'I was sure we'd beaten you when Sebastian skidded into that last ditch, just before the finish.'

'Ah, but the gearbox James Cameron designed soon got us out of trouble!' Angus smiled. 'He's a gifted engineer, that lad. I warn you, Joseph, I intend to lure him back!'

'You can't.'

'Sorry, but I can. I'll offer him a salary he cannot refuse.'

'Then I'll tell you something about James that'll change

your mind!' Joseph cried angrily. 'James Cameron is my son!'

'*Your* son?' Angus paled as he realized the implications. 'You mean that you and Mary-Jane . . . ?'

'Yes. We – we were lovers, Angus.'

That admission silenced Angus for several long moments, then he shook his head and sighed. 'And I branded her a shameless woman!'

The brothers stared at one another.

'So what now?' Joseph asked heavily. 'Will you take my son away from me?'

'I don't know. I don't know what to think any more, to be honest.' Angus turned up his coat collar and huddled unhappily into its warmth. 'Joseph, you must come to the house. We have to talk about this.'

'But won't that upset Mother?'

'Mother's not so fragile as we thought.' Angus smiled grimly. 'Maybe your daughter was just the tonic she needed.'

'Very well.' Joseph made up his mind. 'I'll come tomorrow. I – I can't face any more anguish today . . .' He turned and walked hastily away.

After leaving Sebastian, Gracie headed for the line of cars looking for Evan. To her disappointment, only James was there, tinkering morosely with the wheels.

'Where's Evan?' she asked.

'Gone.'

'What d'you mean, gone?'

'He's gone and left us in the lurch.' He put down a spanner and stared at her. 'I don't know what you've done to him, Gracie, but I've never seen a man so hurt and angry.'

'I haven't done anything!' she cried tearfully.

Then a thought occurred. Had Evan seen Sebastian trying to kiss her? Had he jumped to the wrong conclusion, and minded so much he'd decided to leave? But there was no need! she thought in anguish. It was all a dreadful mistake. She was fond of Sebastian, of course, but she had no illusions about him. Sebastian would always prefer beautiful, well-dressed girls who enjoyed the bright lights of London. He would very soon tire of a female engineer in overalls! Evan was different. Evan was steadfast and loyal. Evan was – Oh, why had he gone away and left her?

She looked wildly round the field.

'Where did he go, James?'

'Over there, see?' He pointed. 'He got on a bus. There! It's just leaving.'

She began to run desperately towards the lumbering vehicle, feet sinking into muddy, trampled ground at every step, slowing her down to a plod. The packed bus lurched out of the field towards the main road. Gracie frantically redoubled her efforts. Her foot caught on a tussock of grass and she went sprawling.

She dragged herself to her knees just in time to watch the bus reach the main road and pick up speed.

'Evan! Evan, come back!' she sobbed uselessly.

People round about had come rushing to her aid, but someone had already run across and picked her up, out of the mud.

'It's all right—' a man's voice was insisting. 'Please – don't cry—!'

But she was so distressed and near to fainting she paid no attention, staring after the bus and struggling to be free.

'Come back! Evan, please, please, come back!'

'Gracie, calm down!' Evan cried. 'I'm still here!'

'Evan?'

Slowly her head cleared. She looked up dazedly to find herself in his arms. She closed her eyes thankfully, leaning against him, both of them soaked and muddy beyond belief.

'Oh, Evan! I thought I'd lost you!'

'And I thought I could leave you! Aren't we the fools?' He grinned. 'I let the bus go without me. I had to see you one last time, I had to ask – oh, Gracie, is there any hope for me with you?'

Gracie gazed at him, suddenly so overcome she couldn't say a word. But she didn't have to tell him what was in her heart and mind. The love and promise in her honest blue eyes was enough for Evan.

The rain had come on again heavily as ever, but he hardly noticed. He threw back his head and laughed.

'I may have lost the race, my love, but I am thinking that maybe I have won the contest.'

Then arm in arm the two of them walked back across the field, quite oblivious of pouring rain, squelching mud – and the knowing grins of spectators . . .

Twelve

The weather was just as changeable in London that Saturday morning. Rosie MacDougal was on her way to Poulter Street to keep an appointment with Edwin Barlow.

She had a fluttery feeling inside, but at least now she knew what an emporium was. Rosie had visited the lending library and spoken to the librarian.

Knowing Edwin's taste for pretty young ladies, the librarian was not what Rosie had expected. Miss Simpkins was fiftyish with greying hair drawn back into a tidy bun. She was very friendly and helpful though, and had recognized Rosie's description of Edwin immediately.

'You mean the charming young man who borrows biographies?'

'That's 'im!'

The motherly librarian didn't know it, but she'd just cleared Rosie's head of stray cobwebs of doubt and settled her future. Edwin was not flirting with a pretty young librarian, as Rosie had imagined. Edwin was revealed as a serious contender for Rosie's heart and hand after months of covert admiration that could easily pass for downright cheek, culminating in a bunch of red roses.

But the library visit had proved to Rosie – if any further proof were really needed – that the choice of her own true love had been extremely wise—

It felt strange approaching Edwin's shop. Last time it

had been evening and it was all lit up, but on this rainy Saturday it looked just as bright. There were lights on inside. A shocking waste of money! Lighting did make the window displays attractive though. Rosie would have liked to linger and look, but she'd no doubt Edwin was keeping an eye open for her.

He was. He held the shop door open. She noted the door was a fancy chromium affair glazed with swirly coloured glass.

'Art Nouveau,' he said nonchalantly, following the direction of her gaze.

'Art who?' Rosie retorted, caustically.

Grandma Hawkins was sitting in a brightly lit bower of flowers. She hugged Rosie delightedly.

'Wonderful to 'ave you back in the fold, luv.'

'It's not official yet, Grandma!'

'It will be once Grandpa's 'ad the board meeting.' Her grandmother beamed.

Hawkins' boardroom made Rosie gasp. Edwin had gone to town on it. There was a huge mahogany table you could see your face in, fancy carved chairs and gold-framed pictures on the walls.

'Meeting will come to order!' Grandpa Hawkins rapped on the table with a dainty little hammer, made special. He cleared his throat importantly. 'We're gathered 'ere today to consider a proposal—'

He paused patiently while Grandma blubbered for a bit then mopped her eyes emotionally, then he went on, 'Miss Rosie MacDougal is proposing an important union which requires the approval of all directors 'ere present.'

''Ear, 'ear, Rosie! Well done, girl!' Grandma whooped excitedly.

'Not yet, luv!' Grandpa shushed. He looked round the table.

'The vote before the Board is for Hawkins' Emporium

and Bertrand's Bakery to form a business partnership – Bertrand's Bakery to supply the store with quality bread, cakes an' tea-bread, all as agreed quite recent by young Mr Bertrand. Those in favour say aye.'

There was a hearty chorus of approval.

'Motion carried h-unanimous!' Grandpa declared with satisfaction.

Rosie gazed around her. Oh, she was so pleased to be back in favour with them all! She rose to her feet and took a deep breath.

'And I've an important announcement to make concerning this here union, Mr Chairman Grandpa,' she said, looking round the interested faces. 'I want you all to know I'm intending to marry young Bertrand. He popped the question yesterday and I said yes.' Rosie's eyes went moist with emotion. 'Bertrand's such a sweetheart, y'see, and I'm so sweet on him we don't 'ave to 'ave a vote. No need for a show of 'ands!'

She smiled softly, remembering how the darling man had gone down on one knee on the spotless bakery floor to propose. When she'd said yes shyly, he'd presented her with a silver dish of iced fancies decorated with red sugar roses. Oh, it was ever so romantic! And the kiss they'd shared after was the sweetest Rosie could imagine . . .

Edwin came round the table, took her hands and kissed her cheek. 'Bertrand's a good bloke, Rosie. I'm happy for you, I really am.' And he sounded as if he really meant it.

The day after the contest at the Glentarn motor rally found Joseph MacDougal approaching the house in which he'd been born. It looked unfamiliar, and he eyed the building with trepidation. It had been little more than an old farmhouse standing beside a busy smithy last time he saw it. Now, surveying the fine property and extensive engineering works today, he had to take his hat off to his brother Angus. He braced himself to meet his mother again with a mixture of eager anticipation and utter dread.

Inside the house, Janet MacDougal was feeling just as jittery and apprehensive as she waited for her son to arrive. To forgive and forget? she wondered.

But who should be doing the forgiving—?

When Joseph was ushered into the drawing room, he noticed that Gracie moved nervously closer to her grandmother as if she needed the old lady's support. It was a significant gesture, he thought. Did she know what happened? Had they told her what he had done?

His gaze took in a beautiful room and rich furnishings, then fell grimly on James Cameron, his son, sitting cosily next to Angus on the sofa.

'I asked Angus if I could come, Joseph.' James shifted uncomfortably under his father's accusing gaze. 'I wanted to tell you myself that I've decided to work with him here in Kelso.'

'So you couldn't resist the grand offer!' Joseph said bitterly.

'That wasn't the main reason,' James retorted. 'My mother needs me here. Besides, I'm not a man that can live in big cities,' he said with genuine regret.

'So where does that leave me?' Joseph sighed dispiritedly.

'I was hoping you'd agree to design sports cars for us, Joseph,' Angus intervened. 'We can build them here in the works and you could sell them from your London garage, where there's more demand from young sporty types.'

'Evan can't keep the repair side of the garage going and attend to car sales without some help.' Joseph shook his head.

'You have a daughter! Why not make use of Gracie's talents?' Angus asked.

'That depends on Gracie,' Joseph said. He glanced at

her. 'I can see you've heard my family's version of the story, Gracie. Do you want to work with me now?'

Janet MacDougal stiffened angrily. 'Is there another version, Joseph?'

'Yes, Mother. There's the truth!'

She sighed wearily. 'I found out today that James Cameron is your son and my grandson, Joseph. After that I'm ready to believe almost anything!'

'Even about Patrick?' Joseph's tone was gentle.

'Patrick—?' His mother looked at him, startled. She had gone pale.

'He was your favourite, wasn't he, Mother?' Joseph persisted. 'I suppose Angus and I both accepted you loved Patrick best. I don't blame you for that. He was so handsome and very charming.' Joseph looked down at her. He went on quietly but deliberately. 'But Patrick had a weakness – and it proved fatal.'

'No, Joseph! Please – no!' the old lady whispered.

'Dad, don't!' Gracie cried, clasping her grandmother's cold hand.

'I'm sorry, Gracie. It had to be said.' Joseph sighed, watching his mother's distress compassionately.

'He . . . he was highly strung, Joseph, that's all . . .' She faltered.

'No, Mother.' He shook his head. 'It was more than that, and maybe deep in your heart you'd always known it. Maybe that's why you gave him extra care and attention. But I trusted Patrick. I even took him into my confidence and begged him to attend to the books so that I could steal away and meet Mary-Jane in our secret hideaway.' Joseph hesitated, then forced himself to go on. 'So you see, in a way I *was* to blame for what happened. I gave Patrick the opportunity. He was clever with figures. It was easy for him to alter the accounts, falsify ledger entries, steal the money and cover his tracks.'

213

'No! Patrick wouldn't do that!' His mother wept. 'He had a very generous allowance and when he asked, I gave him more.'

'Even that wasn't enough!' Joseph shook his head sadly. 'He was betting on horses and gambling heavily at cards. Gambling was an obsession with him. I discovered later that he'd owed large sums to money-lenders, and they wanted it back – with interest.'

'Poor boy! Poor boy!' His mother covered her face with her hands and sobbed.

'But how did you find out he was robbing the firm?' Angus frowned.

'He'd altered accounts which I happened to know were wrong. I checked up and was stunned to find out how much he'd embezzled. I met him down by the river and challenged him with theft. He admitted what he'd done, but threatened to tell Father that I planned to marry Mary-Jane and had stolen the money to keep her in the style to which she was accustomed!'

Joseph couldn't go on, the memories of that day were so traumatic. He imagined he could still hear an echo of his young brother's threats ringing in his ears.

'He taunted me.' Joseph's voice shook. 'I was furious . . . !'

'Did you attack him? Did you push him in?' Angus cried.

'No! I did not!' He stared at his brother. 'Angus, think about it! You must know I could never do that. It . . . it's not in my nature to do it. Patrick wanted to get his version of the story to Father first. He knew he was the favoured one and there was a good chance he'd be believed. But in his hurry, he slipped—'

There was a deathly hush in the pleasant room. The old lady had stopped weeping and sat in frozen silence.

Joseph went to her and took her hands in his.

'You wouldn't believe me. You wouldn't hear a word

against him. You were devastated and brokenhearted and you said cruel and terrible things to me,' he told her, '—and I took it all. I took the blame in an attempt to ease your grief, because I loved you, Mother.' Joseph sighed and shook his head. 'But it was mistaken kindness! I can see that now. I should have forced you to face the truth about Patrick. I should have stuck to my guns and cleared my name. It might have saved this family years of misery and strife.'

'But Dad,' Gracie cried suddenly, 'your life would have been quite different if you had. You wouldn't have met and married Mum, and I wouldn't be here today!'

She ran to her father and hugged him. Joseph held his daughter in his arms thankfully and there was silence while the MacDougal family contemplated the strange twists and turns of fate that had brought them all together in this room.

Presently Janet MacDougal straightened her back, wiped her eyes, and regained composure.

'Joseph, my son, I'm deeply sorry.' She looked at him with humility and a hint of hope. 'Can you ever forgive me?'

'Of course I can!' He laughed and kissed her.

Wordlessly, she patted his cheek. Then she rose stiffly and crossed to the bureau. The old lady opened a drawer and took out a silver-framed photograph of her three handsome sons. She studied it fondly for a moment then quietly, with pride and sorrow, Janet MacDougal placed the photograph of her sons upon the mantelshelf, in full view . . .

September at last!

Polly, dressed in wedding finery, took a final hurried glance out of the window. September weather was a lottery, and the only wedding detail outside Polly's control. But it looked as if the Almighty had turned up trumps for Lily and

Matthew's wedding. There were blue skies and fluffy white clouds and no wind to speak of to ruffle fine feathers.

'You look lovely, Polly!' her husband said admiringly.

'You don't look too bad yourself, luv.' She smiled archly.

Lovingly, she straightened his tie. Joseph looked handsome and distinguished in morning suit and grey waistcoat. His health had improved and he wore a confident prosperous air these days, now that the garage was doing well.

He would have kissed her, but she squealed.

'Joseph, mind me lipstick!'

Laughing, she went into the girls' room. It was like a jumble sale in there, everyday clothes tossed on the beds and the dressing table littered with pots and potions. The room was scented like a perfumery.

The three girls were dressed and ready, though. They were standing in a little group by the window in the sunlight, clothed in silk and with fresh flowers in their shining hair.

'Mum, how do we look?' Rosie cried happily.

Polly just stood there. What could she say? How could she possibly describe how she felt, looking at them now? She only knew she would carry this radiant picture of her beloved daughters with her till the day she died.

She swallowed tears.

'You look perfect, my darlings. Just perfect!' she told them.

After that, Polly had to get a move on. She always walked to church and saw no reason to change a habit for a wedding. Joseph and the girls would drive in impressive style in a magnificent Austin 20 landaulet which Evan had hired as his wedding gift.

Evan was a fine, steady man and he and Gracie were a great help to Joseph. There would be another wedding there one day, Polly thought. But there was time enough for that. Gracie was young and ambitious and planned to gain an engineering qualification at college first, then go into business with her dad and Evan.

Heads turned as Polly walked by, but she scarcely noticed. She was preoccupied, running over the arrangements in her head. It had been an inspired thought by Matthew to ask James Cameron to be his best man. Rosie and Lily were finding it easier now to accept James as a brother.

Turning her mind to the guest list, Polly smiled. She'd instructed the ushers that all the Scottish guests – Joseph's mother, his brother Angus and Mary-Jane Cameron – were to be shown to the front pew beside Grandma and Grandpa Hawkins. Hawkins relatives could be counted upon to put on a lively show in the second row. Matthew's East Enders were an unknown quantity but still, the hymn-singing should be lusty!

The wedding cake! Well, that would be a triumph in young Bertrand's hands. Rosie's fiancé planned four tiers, decorated with sugar lilies. What with that and the reception feast Matthew's capable foster mother had planned in the Bright Street church hall, Polly was sure everyone's eyes would sparkle.

She came within sight of the church and saw the East End crowds flocking in decorously, dressed in their best, bless 'em all.

Edwin Barlow was standing in the doorway when Polly arrived at the church. He was escorting a pretty young lady she'd never seen before. Edwin made the introductions with an amused gleam in his eye.

'Miss Amy Wiggins, my Aunt Polly. Amy's a librarian. Been a great help to me, Amy has.'

'But Rosie told me the librarian was . . .' Polly stared at the pretty girl in astonishment.

'Oh yes, I know,' said Edwin blandly. 'Rosie met old

Miss Simpkins in Lending, but Amy works in Reference, you see.'

Beneath his usual jaunty appearance, his happiness was transparent. Polly was relieved to know Rosie hadn't broken Edwin's heart – any more than Gracie had broken Sebastian's, it seemed.

For there was Sebastian with his latest girlfriend, walking behind Lady Frances, assisted by her husband's arm. Polly was delighted to note that those two older ones looked as happy together as she was herself, with her dear Joseph. At last the past was behind them.

Oh, the future did look bright . . . !

But it was time for the bride's mother to make an entrance. Polly straightened her hat and walked in stately fashion down the aisle. From the corner of an eye she checked that Grandma's lovely flowers were arranged to perfection and everything in place down to the smallest detail. She could relax and enjoy a wonderful wedding. She might even let slip a few happy tears.

Polly smiled mistily at Grandma Hawkins, resplendent in emerald green. Lovingly, she kissed her mother's cheek.

'Everything all right, luvvie?' Grandpa leaned across.

'Perfect, Pa!' whispered Polly.

Just as the congregation rose, the organ pealed out 'Here Comes the Bride', and her lovely daughters and handsome husband began their walk down the aisle, five modest minutes late, just as Polly had planned . . .